The Lie Direct

THE LIE DIRECT

Sara Woods

The retort courteous . . . the quip modest . . . the reply
churlish . . . the reproof valiant . . . the countercheck
quarrelsome . . . the lie circumstantial . . . the lie direct.

As You Like It, Act V, scene iv

St. Martin's Press
New York

Any work of fiction whose characters were of uniform excellence would rightly be condemned—by that fact if by no other—as being incredibly dull. Therefore no excuse can be considered necessary for the villainy or folly or the people appearing in this book. It seems extremely unlikely that any of them should resemble a real person, alive or dead. Any such resemblance is completely unintentional and without malice.

S.W.

Library of Congress Cataloging in Publication Data

Woods, Sara, pseud.
  The lie direct.

  I. Title.
PR6073.063L5   1983   823'.914   83-2982
ISBN 0-312-48369-4

First published in Great Britain by Macmillan London Limited.

First U.S. Edition

10 9 8 7 6 5 4 3 2 1

PROLOGUE

MONDAY, March 11th

I

'It's all very well, Geoffrey,' said Antony Maitland, and Geoffrey Horton, a solicitor friend of long standing who was desirous at the moment of offering him a brief, looked visibly downcast by what he considered an inauspicious beginning, 'you're asking me to defend a man who's obviously guilty —'

Don't be naïve, Antony,' Geoffrey told him crossly. 'It's news to me that all your clients are innocent.'

'— and on a charge of treason too,' Maitland continued, ignoring the interruption as irrelevant, as perhaps it was. 'Yes, I know your instructions are to plead Not Guilty, but the best you seem able to come up with by way of a defence is to say, like Pooh Bah, "I wasn't there." '

'Which is quite a good defence if it can be proved,' said Geoffrey reasonably. 'In any case, the chap's been charged under the Official Secrets Act.'

'That's only a technicality, and you know it. A man who betrays his country —'

'You defended Guy Harland, and that was treason.'

'That was ten years ago.'

'Twelve,' said Geoffrey, who had a maddening habit of accuracy.

'All right then, twelve. And look what happened. He said it was a case of mistaken identity too, and then changed his

30062

mind half-way through the trial.'

'He didn't change his plea of Not Guilty.'

'No,' admitted Antony grudgingly.

'Which proved to be the right one. But the two cases are completely dissimilar,' said Geoffrey briskly.

'Guy Harland was innocent, even though he lied about who he was at first. That makes a difference . . . don't you think?'

'My instructions —'

'Damn your instructions,' said Maitland, exasperated. 'Do *you* believe this story that you're expecting me to produce in court?'

'Well . . . no. That is, not exactly.'

'There you are then!' It didn't suit him at the momemt to take note of the slight hesitation in Geoffrey's reply. 'Give me one good reason', he went on, 'why I should accept the brief, and I won't argue any further.'

'Because I'd like you to,' said Horton unequivocally.

'But —' For the moment Maitland was visibly taken aback by the very simplicity of the statement. 'But why would you like me to?' he persisted.

'I realise it's an imposition to ask you to take it on at this late date,' said Geoffrey, which may have been a way of avoiding the question. In any event Maitland brushed the remark aside impatiently.

'There's no need for that kind of talk between you and me,' he said. 'I realise that if Kevin O'Brien hadn't had an emergency appendectomy —'

'His last words as they wheeled him into the operating theatre', said Geoffrey, with uncharacteristic drama, 'were "Get hold of Maitland." '

'Kevin is notably sympathetic towards lost causes,' said Antony unimpressed.

'Wouldn't you say the same thing applied to you?'

Maitland considered that. 'Perhaps it does, but in a different degree,' he admitted. But he hesitated over his

6

next remark, a fact that was only too obvious to someone who knew him as well as Geoffrey did.

'Something on your mind, Antony,' he said accusingly. 'It can't be your work-load, in spite of the short notice I'm giving you —'

'No notice at all,' Antony amended amiably.

'— because Mallory told me that one of your clients whose case was just due to come up had left suddenly for parts unknown, leaving no address.'

Maitland grinned at that. 'True enough,' he said. 'It happens, and in this case, from my client's point of view, it was the best thing he could possibly have done. However that isn't quite the point.'

'What is the point, then?'

'There's a complication you don't know about, Geoffrey.'

'Hadn't you better tell me about it, then?'

'Yes, of course. I'm going to. It's this chap Gollnow.'

'Dr Boris Gollnow?'

'Precisely. The chap whose defection the papers have been full of for the past few weeks.'

'Well, what about him?'

'He was ostensibly attached to the Russian Embassy, but actually he was a specialist from Directorate T.'

'That wasn't made public, but I don't see what difference it makes. I don't even know what it means,' said Horton frankly.

'That doesn't matter at the moment, except for the fact that when he asked for political asylum he was able to offer the authorities a *quid pro quo*.'

'Yes, I know that; information about Nesbit and Ryder.'

'That's not what I meant. Something very secret and technical. The trouble is that no one knows whether to believe him.'

'That won't, unfortunately, affect his impressiveness as a witness against John Ryder.'

'Don't be so single-minded, Geoffrey. The thing is, I've been asked to sit in on one or two of the questioning sessions to see what I make of him.'

'But that's insane.' Geoffrey was indignant. 'If ever there was a chap who knew nothing about technical matters —'

'Less than nothing,' Maitland agreed.

'And anyway you don't speak Russian,' said Geoffrey, as though that clinched matters.

'It isn't a question of languages this time. Obviously he's fluent in English or he wouldn't have been at the Embassy here. The trouble is, Geoffrey, ever since that business in New York the powers that be seem to have got the idea that I've only to look at a chap to tell whether he's lying or not. I only wish it were true,' he added, rather ruefully.

'You might have told me that at the beginning,' said Horton.

'And saved you the trouble of putting up all those arguments? I haven't agreed to the suggestion, and I don't feel under any obligation to do so, because quite frankly I don't think it would do any good.'

'Well then, you're free to take the case,' said Geoffrey eagerly. 'And it will get you off the hook with whoever it is who's importuning you, because nobody could possibly expect you to act in both capacities.'

'No, they couldn't, could they?' Antony was smiling at his friend's eagerness, though he had some mental reservations as to the truth of that statement. 'And I admit it's the best of reasons, to get you out of the hole Kevin's illness has left you in.'

'Suppose John Ryder is innocent,' said Horton. 'That would be an even more cogent one.'

'Don't tell me you're falling into old Bellerby's ways.' Mr Bellerby, that eminent solicitor noted for his insistence on kindness to clients, was Horton's father-in-law.

Geoffrey ignored the question. 'No, but supposing he is,' he insisted.

8

'You've got some reason for saying that. And now I come to think of it, you were a bit hesitant just now when I asked you whether you believed his story.'

'Well, I didn't, but — you've told me this often enough, Antony — I'm not the judge and jury.'

'Neither am I. But that isn't the whole of it, is it?'

'No. The thing is, Mrs Ryder came to see me.'

'That was extremely improper of her, considering that she's one of the chief witnesses for the prosecution.'

'I don't mean that Mrs Ryder. The other one,' said Geoffrey, rather less lucidly than was usual with him.

'Oh, I see. Hadn't you approached her to see if there was anything that could be said in extenuation?'

'No, Ryder insisted that I leave her out of it. She's expecting a baby . . . any minute from the look of her,' he added inconsequently, 'and I suppose he thought she might be upset. But I've also got the idea that he felt she wouldn't believe his story either, and wouldn't be willing to testify on his behalf.'

'But she is?'

'For what it's worth, yes. And as to her husband's character, and the closeness of their relationship, she was oddly convincing.'

'Even to an old cynic like you.'

'If you like to put it that way. The thing is that she says she handled all the family finances. Even when they were hard up, which happened sometimes during the last year, since the baby was coming and she had given up her job, he never attempted to — to make an extra contribution. Which he could have done, you know, if he'd had income from another source, by telling her some tale about a bonus from the firm, something like that.'

'Nobody's saying that he paid for the London flat himself, at least not out of the salary he earned from his regular job.'

'No, but . . . well, it's a point anyway,' said Geoffrey

9

stubbornly. 'The thing is, Antony, she's a nice girl and deserves a break.'

'Are you so sure it would be a break to return her husband to her? And that raises another point, Geoffrey, I'm not at all clear which of these two women your client seems to have married is the real Mrs Ryder.'

'The one I'm talking about. Her name's Caroline but Ryder always calls her Carol. They were married three years ago, at least six months before the other ceremony took place.'

'Doesn't she mind being married to a bigamist?'

'She doesn't think she is. She believes implicitly everything he says.'

'And you're in two minds about it,' said Maitland thoughtfully. 'All right, Geoffrey, I'll do what you want, but only to help you out, not because I believe a word of this rigmarole. Can I talk to Kevin?'

'Not today at any rate; they only operated this morning. And as there's every likelihood we shall be in court tomorrow.' (Antony groaned but made no other comment) 'you'll just have to read your brief for once.'

'I always do,' said Maitland automatically. Geoffrey had his briefcase open and was reverently laying an unwieldy pile of papers on the desk. 'Is that all?' asked Antony in an awestruck tone. 'I suppose you realise I shall be up all night.'

'It won't be the first time,' said Geoffrey heartlessly. 'Do you want to see Ryder in the morning?'

'Not particularly. Is all this prosecution evidence?'

'All except for the Ryders' statements, and one or two other oddments.'

'Then it looks as if I shall see more than enough of the gentleman in the next few days.'

Geoffrey was on his feet, watching as the documents were transferred into Antony's own briefcase. 'You'll see from that', he said, 'that we haven't a hope of proving that th

10

information handed over wasn't prejudicial.'

'No use calling for part of the hearing to be held in camera while we go into it?'

'None at all — are you coming home now?' Geoffrey asked.

'In a moment. I've got to communicate my decision not to help interview Gollnow to somebody. After that —'

'Then I'll see you here in the morning if that's all right with you. About nine thirty? I should know by then what business the court has to get through before they reach us.'

'Nine thirty it is.' As Geoffrey went out he was pulling the telephone towards him. 'You won't expect me to be word-perfect by then,' he called after him. 'I'm what Meg would call a slow study.'

Geoffrey was smiling as he made his own way out. He was pretty sure he knew better than that.

II

That talk had taken place in Sir Nicholas Harding's chambers in the Inner Temple, of which Maitland was a member. Since he was also Sir Nicholas's nephew their association was not merely a professional one, and in fact he and his wife, Jenny, occupied the two top floors of Sir Nicholas's house in Kempenfeldt Square.

The arrangement had been made temporarily many years before, as a matter of expediency, but none of them chose to remember that now. Only one person had joined the household since Antony and Jenny were married; Sir Nicholas had taken to wife, nearly three years ago now, the former Miss Vera Langhorne, barrister-at-law, and this — whichever way you looked at it — was to all of them a distinct gain. Not only did they love Vera for herself, but she had proved to have the most excellent influence over Sir Nicholas's underworked and overbearing staff; so that

11

though Gibbs, the butler, for whose retirement they had all prayed for years, still enjoyed playing the role of a martyr to duty, it was perhaps with not quite the ostentation he had displayed before.

However he still lurked in the hall of an evening until he was sure that everyone was home, and that evening was no exception; but beyond remarking, 'You're late this evening, Mr Maitland,' — the inference being, of course, that this was in some way an act of gross inconsideration for others — he allowed Antony to go upstairs to his own quarters without comment.

Though their place was by no means self-contained, the Maitlands did have their own front door on the second-floor landing. When the house was originally being divided, all sorts of rules as to procedure had been set up, but Antony couldn't remember now that any of them had ever been kept, and certainly it was many years since the door had been locked, except on one occasion which for reasons of his own he preferred not to think about. Eventually, however, it had developed a characteristic squeak, which on the whole they found convenient, so that now, when Jenny heard it she came immediately into the hall. 'I thought that man running away had left you with some time to spare,' she said, 'but I don't call this early.'

'Now, love, I had enough of that from Gibbs downstairs,' Antony protested. 'And I'm afraid the position's been completely reversed. Geoffrey has a case he wants me to take on at short notice . . . or rather at no notice at all because we shall probably be in court tomorrow.'

'That isn't like him.' He was tired, she could see that. After all, the Hilary term was already well advanced, and it couldn't exactly be said that it had been an easy one. That, however, was one of the things she had arranged with herself long since never to mention. Instead, 'Come in and I'll get you a drink,' she invited. 'You needn't hurry yourself, dinner won't spoil. And now,' she went on, after she had provided him with sherry, curled up in her own favourite corner of the sofa, and had seen Antony's drink placed on the mantel bedside the clock, 'what's Geoffrey wished on you this time?'

'Defending a man called John Ryder.'

'The one who's connected with that Russian?'

'The very same. Kevin O'Brien was doing it, but he's in hospital having just had his appendix out.'

'Why didn't Geoffrey ask you in the first place?'

'Because I'm pretty sure Kevin would have put on a better show than I shall.'

'That's nonsense, Antony, and you know it.'

Maitland shook his head. '*The great Gaels of Ireland,*' he said, as though that explained everything.

'What on earth do you mean?' asked Jenny incredulously.

'*For the great Gaels of Ireland*', Antony repeated obligingly, '*are the men the Gods made mad. For all their wars are merry, and all their songs are sad.* Not that the last two lines are strictly relevant,' he added reflectively.

'I suppose I see,' said Jenny doubtfully. 'Why Geoffrey wanted him, I mean. But I *am* a bit surprised that you agreed.'

'I probably shouldn't have done if he'd approached me in the first place. As it is, it's a difficult situation for him. He's got to find somebody, and you know, love, we owe Geoffrey a good deal one way and another.'

'Yes, I know. Only I don't want you to take on anything that worries you.'

'It won't worry me in the slightest, I can promise you that, at least not in the way you mean. But there's a pile of papers in my briefcase to be got through tonight, because, as I said, there's every liklihood the case will be reached tomorrow, and so far I don't know a thing about it except that Halloran is prosecuting, and that we haven't a defence . . . except for Ryder's denials, of course.'

13

'In that case I don't see any point in your reading through the papers at all,' said Jenny, smiling at him. He was standing in his favourite place, a little to the side of the the fire, and now he turned to pick up his glass, a tall man with dark hair, a thin, intelligent face, and rather more humour and rather more sensitivity in his make-up than was good for him. Now, turning back again and finding her grey eyes fixed on him a little anxiously, he returned her smile and thought as he did so that without Jenny's serenity there were times when life would be almost impossibly difficult.

'There's one other thing,' he said as lightly as he could. 'Our client seems to be a bigamist.'

'The papers haven't been too informative,' said Jenny.

'Not because of the bigamy,' Antony assured her.

'No, of course not. I know better than that. It would be contempt of court to comment on a case that's *sub judice*,' said Jenny wisely. 'All the same I got the impression . . . I mean, there's quite a lot they could have said without going into anything — anything classified, isn't there?'

'Better be sure than sorry,' Antony told her, without any great originality. 'I gather from what I know already that there are aspects of Gollnow's information that shouldn't be made public property.'

'I see,' said Jenny doubtfully. 'Does that mean you won't be able to talk to us about it?'

Maitland laughed at that, though it evoked memories that gave him no pleasure at all. 'My dearest love, I don't suppose anything profoundly secret will be spoken of in open court,' he told her.

'Well, I suppose the law knows its own business best,' said Jenny. 'I suppose this man of yours is pleading Not Guilty.'

'Geoffrey wouldn't have been in such a stew about finding somebody to defend him if he weren't.'

'No, that's true. Does Geoffrey believe him?'

'I think Geoffrey is going a bit soft in his old age,' Antony

14

told her. 'As far as I can make out he doesn't *exactly* believe him, but isn't at all sure that he disbelieves him either. The chap has a very attractive wife apparently.'

'Which one? Which of the wives, I mean?'

'Both of them, for all I know. I'm talking about the real wife, the one he lived with in Wolverhampton, not the one in the flat in town.'

'Oh dear, how terribly confusing.'

'It is, isn't it?' He finished his drink, refilled both their glasses, and instead of taking his usual chair came to sit beside her on the sofa. 'But it's nothing for you to worry about, love,' he assured her. 'Even if I wanted to meddle, as Uncle Nick calls it, I wouldn't have time . . . would I now?'

'I suppose not.' But Jenny still sounded doubtful. 'So there's nothing whatever about the case that Uncle Nick can object to,' she added more cheerfully, after a moment's reflection.

'Nothing at all, love,' he assured her. 'Except insofar', he added, in the interests of accuracy, 'as Uncle Nick can find something to complain of in almost anything if he really sets his mind to it.'

15

REGINA *versus* RYDER (1974)

THE CASE FOR THE PROSECUTION

TUESDAY, the first day of the trial

I

The trial was to be held in the Number One Court of the Old Bailey, and it was odd, Maitland thought, sitting decorously in his place and waiting for the judge to appear, how much more solemn the occasion seemed than even a trial for so serious a matter as murder. Perhaps, even in these degenerate times, there was a built-in sense of patriotism in the man-in-the-street. The silence, for instance, was almost complete, no shuffling or coughing or the turning of the pages of reporters' notebooks.

To turn to more important matters, Bruce Halloran Q.C., a formidable prosecutor at any time, was obviously in this instance quite sure that he had all the facts at his fingertips. He too was sitting quietly in his place and the books and papers in front of him were undisturbed. Next to him his learned friend Mr Hawthorne was equally relaxed.

Nor did the defence team do anything to detract from the general atmosphere. Maitland had undergone — half amused, half irritated — a cross-examination from his instructing solicitor earlier that morning as to the results of his study of his brief and the accompanying papers. He had also had the chance to talk to his junior, Derek Stringer, who had been in the affair from the beginning. Derek was an old friend, and also in Sir Nicholas's chambers, so Antony knew he could rely on him implicitly to keep him on the right track if he strayed from the straight and narrow. 'The only thing that puzzles me', he had said at the meeting, 'is that Ryder thinks it's worth while putting on a defence at all. Why not plead Guilty and have done with it?'

Stringer had shrugged at that. He was a man not easily excited, and if he was relieved that on this occasion his leader showed no sign of mounting a crusade he gave no evidence of it. He would, Maitland knew, follow where he led without question and without complaint, and also without expressing in any way his own opinion of the matter in hand.

Professionally speaking, he wasn't too sorry that Halloran had the prosecution. If he was going to go down in defeat, as seemed almost certain, it might as well be to a first class opponent. True, Halloran was an old friend of his uncle's, and the trial that was about to open would probably provide material for pleasantries for many months to come, but he didn't see any way of avoiding that. On the whole, too, he was glad that Mr Justice Carruthers would be trying the case. He was a fair-minded man, and never as impatient as some of his brethren on the bench were if counsel introduced any matter that might be considered unorthodox. Not that Antony foresaw the need for introducing any fireworks in this business, it was only too straightforward.

And now, here was Mr Justice Carruthers, looking no older than he had done years ago when Maitland first appeared before him, one of those men who didn't seem to age because they have never looked really young. He was a small man whom Maitland always thought of as having a face like an intelligent bloodhound; and if that was a disrespectful description, the fault, he thought, was in himself and not in the judge.

Carruthers for his part, seating himself and taking his time to look about him, had been informed of course that Maitland would be appearing in Kevin O'Brien's place —

to oblige his friend Horton, no doubt, and for no other reason. It would be interesting, thought the judge, with a little gentle malice, to see what he made of a quite hopeless situation. (And lest it be thought that his lordship was guilty of pre-judging the matter, let it be said immediately that he had formed this opinion solely from Bruce Halloran's rather smug appearance, which meant without any doubt at all that the prosecution was very sure of its case. But there were the facts to be presented, and to these he would listen with a completely open mind.) And there was Derek Stringer too, a good foil for his more volatile leader, a very tall man, bald before his time, whose effects in the robing-room, the judge knew, included a hair-piece that he had taken off when he had assumed his wig.

Bruce Halloran, naturally, was also well known to his lordship. There would be no surprises there; he would conduct the prosecution competently, sometimes almost savagely, and yet without for a moment forfeiting the sympathy of the jury. He was a big man, very dark of complexion, which in wig and bands was especially evident. And to match his size he had a big voice, most of the time consciously held in check, but capable too of booming out through the courtroom in an exceedingly impressive way.

The jury, oddly enough — or perhaps, after all, it was only to be expected — looked rather more uneasy and self-conscious than usual. Which was all right and proper. The defendant, who had popped up in the dock with two warders like a trio of jacks-in-the-box, was a pleasant-looking man, not at all what you would have thought . . . but there, young people today had some very strange ideas. The offence with which he was charged was one which his lordship found particularly distasteful, though he was a charitable enough man to realise that it might have been committed in good faith. The question of two wives, however, though not strictly relevant, was a different matter. But here again the morals of the younger

21

generation . . .

But the indictment had been read, and it was time to turn his attention to Halloran's opening remarks. Mr Justice Carruthers picked up the fountain-pen which it was his clerk's first duty each morning to fill, and assumed an air of alert interest, noting at the same time out of the corner of his eye that Maitland, true to his habit, had slid down in his seat and appeared to be disposing himself for slumber.

If he had not in fact been listening almost as intently as the judge, Antony thought he had gained enough from his reading — which in fact had occupied him until the early hours of the morning in spite of Geoffrey's expressed doubts in that respect — to have been able to deliver Halloran's opening speech, if not word for word, at least quite capably. Even so it was up to him to listen carefully. There was quite likely to be some angle he had missed, something that Halloran's more leisured study of the facts had revealed. But like the judge he had been interested to see the prisoner for the first time, and now was conscious of a small distraction from Halloran's carefully muted phrases in the temptation to consider more carefully what he had seen.

Or perhaps, not such a small temptation, because annoyingly the first words that had come into his head on seeing John Ryder had been: *a commonplace type with a stick and a pipe and a half-bred black and tan*, so that now Sullivan's music and Gilbert's jingle formed an inescapable background to his thoughts. Not that Ryder was a bad-looking fellow: well-set-up, that was the phrase, with a pleasantly rugged face and wiry brown hair. It was just that he looked . . . ordinary. Not an idealist, certainly not a fool. But the last man you would have thought of in connection with the deliberate betrayal of his country. It was probably at this point that the idea first occured to Maitland that it was important that he talked to his client himself, though later he was to rationalise this by insisting both to Derek and Geoffrey that his decision to do so was the

22

result of listening to Boris Gollnow's testimony.

'. . . it may seem to you, members of the jury,' — Halloran was well into his stride by now — 'that an offence committed in peace-time is in some ways less grave than if our country were actually at war. His lordship himself will instruct you on the legalities of the situation when the time comes, but before we go into the question of the prisoner's culpability there are one or two points it may be as well to get quite clear. The Official Secrets Act of 1911 has been supplemented by later acts in 1920 and 1939, though in practice the three are treated as one body of law. A point covered is the obtaining, collecting or communication to any other person of any document or information which is calculated to be, or which might directly or indirectly be, useful to an enemy. There is legal precedent for construing the word enemy to mean a potential enemy with whom we might some day be at war, and also for the fact that the publication of such classified information shall be deemed to be for a purpose prejudicial to the safety or interests of the state unless the contrary is proved. There is one other point which it will be necessary for you to remember in considering the evidence as it is placed before you, and that is that all persons who aid, abet, counsel or procure the offence are to be treated as principal offenders.

'Now, briefly, to the sorry tale of John Ryder's involvement in this unhappy affair. We shall be placing evidence before you to confirm the facts I am about to adduce and it will be for you to weigh this evidence, assess its value, and come to a decision. But I have to tell you now that I am confident that in this matter there can be only one verdict, that of Guilty as charged.

'The facts first came to light when Dr Boris Gollnow of the Russian Embassy approached the authorities here to ask for political asylum. His first approach, in fact, was made to a former British diplomat, an acquaintance who had worked for some years before his retirement in the British Embassy

23

in Moscow. Dr Gollnow's story was — I am putting it in the simplest terms, members of the jury, so that later when we get into the hands of the experts you may not be as confused as I was on first reading the evidence — that his real function in this country was the collection of technical information for his government, and that through the agency of John Ryder he had been put in touch with a man called Dennis Nesbit, now deceased, who had been able to give him particulars of certain work that was going on at present on this country.

'Dr Gollnow had, as I say, been introduced to this man by the prisoner, John Ryder, and all their interviews had taken place at Ryder's London home. I stress that, members of the jury, because Ryder's business — he is a contract administrator for a firm of defence contractors — brought him to London on an average of one week in three. To take advantage of this situation it seems that he had — if I may use the expression — a wife in every port; a wife of three years' standing in Wolverhampton, and another woman who believed herself to be married to him in the flat he rented in London. This lady I suppose we should refer to by her maiden name, Winifred Paull, as it seems the ceremony in her case did not take place until six months after the first. I should like to make it clear immediately that no blame attaches to either of these ladies — perhaps it would not be too strong to call them victims. There is no indication at all that they had any information as to Ryder's activities outside the law.

'Because you may feel that of the two British subjects involved Dennis Nesbit was the more culpable, let me repeat again that a person who procures an offence is to be treated as a principal offender. But even if that were not the case there is no doubt here of John Ryder's guilt. In the London flat was found a photocopying machine, the most expensive of its kind, and a locked, fireproof filing-cabinet containing facsimiles of documents that had obviously been brought by Nesbit to be copied. With his lordship's permission you will hear in evidence this man's dying statement, in which he admits his guilt, and names John Ryder as his accomplice. The same John Ryder, there can be no doubt about that from the particulars given of his work and his lifestyle. In addition to which Dr Gollnow and the — shall I say the second Mrs Ryder? — have both identified him.

'But I feel that this is all I need to tell you.' (At this point Stringer dug Maitland in the ribs and muttered, 'He doesn't want to make his lordship late for lunch.') 'You will hear the whole ugly story repeated to you in more detail by the witnesses we shall call, so it is unnecessary for me to detain you any longer. I will only remind you that it is a foul crime of which John Ryder is accused,' — up to then he had been speaking softly, or as softly as he could, but now his voice rang out through the courtroom — 'a crime against the state, and therefore a crime against each one of us. For which of you does not have someone, be it husband, brother or child, who would be at risk in the event of hostilities. Forgive my emotion,' he concluded, controlling himself with an obvious effort, 'on all these matters you must judge for yourselves.'

'Old humbug,' said Maitland *sotto voce*, opening his eyes. Derek had been quite right. They had started so late that Curruthers decided to take the luncheon recess at that point rather than call the first witness. The defence team went together to Astroff's, but so far there was really nothing to be said about the case and their talk concerned other matters. Only Antony was inclined to be thoughtful.

II

The next witness, whom Maitland found himself eyeing rather warily, was a spry, grey-haired gentleman, perhaps

25

in his late sixties, who gave his name as Charles Daniell and an address in a Sussex village. Bruce Halloran had lowered his voice to as near to a coo as was possible for him.

'You lived in Russia I believe, Sir Charles, from the year 1967 until your retirement two years ago?'

'That is correct. I was a member of the Embassy staff.' (Antony found himself wondering just what activities those innocent words had covered.) 'And when you say Russia, Mr Halloran, I think we should qualify that and specify that I was mostly in Moscow. Too much travel is never popular, and particularly in the last year I was there, after the expulsion of so many members of the K.G.B. and G.R.U. from Britain, it was a matter of treading very warily indeed.'

'Yes, Sir Charles, I think we all understand that,' said Counsel for the Prosecution, obviously — to Maitland's eyes at least — not caring in the least whether the jury knew anything of the matter or not. 'During those years you did, I imagine, make a number of acquaintances in Moscow.'

'Certainly I did. I think you mean among the Russians, and a certain amount of socialising went with the territory as it were.'

'And was one of those acquaintances a Dr Boris Gollnow?'

'I knew him, yes, as well as I knew any of his countrymen. He left Moscow in 1970 to join their Embassy here in London.'

'And after your retirement?'

'Neither my wife nor I care for life in a large city. A small country town, offering the facilities we may need as we grow older and at the same time giving a quick access to the countryside seemed a reasonable compromise.' He paused, smiling. 'That isn't what you want to know, is it, Mr Halloran? You want to know whether I met Dr Gollnow again.'

Halloran cast a rather apologetic look at the judge and

then said smoothly, 'I should like to know, Sir Charles, when you saw Dr Gollnow again after your return to England.'

'Not until he came to see me a month ago.'

'Can you remember the exact date, Sir Charles?'

'Yes I can as a matter of fact. It was the tenth of February, and I remember because it was the day the miners went on strike.'

'Yes, I see. That certainly would have the effect of fixing it in your mind. He visited you at home I take it?'

'Yes, he came there. He wanted my advice on obtaining political asylum in this country. And he told me —'

'Yes, Sir Charles, Dr Gollnow will be giving evidence about that information himself. Perhaps you could tell us now what action you took in consequence of the revelations he made to you.'

'There was only one thing to do, and that was to get in touch with the S.I.S.' ('The Special Intelligence Service, my lord,' said Halloran in a quick aside) 'which I did without delay. They took it from there, though Dr Gollnow stayed with me until someone could arrive to take charge of him. A matter of security, you understand.'

'I see. Now perhaps we may go over the dates again, Sir Charles, so that they are firmly fixed in our minds. You say your tour of duty in Moscow . . .'

The reiteration did not take long. 'That is all I have to ask you then, Sir Charles,' said Halloran, still managing to keep his voice at a reasonable level. 'Unless my learned friend, Mr Maitland, has some questions for you.'

There was an undertone of not unkindly sarcasm in that, at which Antony would have liked to be able to smile openly. So many of his uncle's friends were still inclined to treat him as they had treated the thirteen-year-old who joined Sir Nicholas's bachelor establishment so many years ago after his father's death. But he was used to it, and old enough not to resent it any longer.

'There's not much I wish to ask Sir Charles to add to his very clear testimony,' he said coming to his feet and waiting for a moment until the witness turned to face him. 'Only, as you were talking with my friend, I wondered, sir, whether anything in your acquaintance with Dr Gollnow in Moscow led you to believe that he might wish to defect?'

'No, I can't say that it did.' The witness took the time to turn the matter over in his mind. 'Unless it was that he had a sense of humour,' he added, as though suddenly struck by an inspiration.

At that Maitland allowed his smile to broaden. He was conscious of a sympathy between himself and the witness and for some reason was quite sure that his amusement would not be misunderstood. To use a phrase of Jenny's, Sir Charles Daniell was the sort of man he'd have liked to invite to dinner. 'I wonder if you could explain that for us,' he invited.

'That's not so easy.' Sir Charles was relaxed now, more relaxed than he had been under direct examination. 'I'm not at all sure I understand it myself,' he went on, 'and I wouldn't like you to think that the man in the street in Russia is altogether without humour. "Black humour" I believe it's called nowadays. There are stories in the press sometimes of the latest *on dit* in Moscow, that I can't recall at the moment —'

'Yes, I've seen them too,' said Maitland as the witness's voice trailed off. 'And I can't remember any of them either. But I know what you mean.'

'It seems to me', said the judge, coming to life suddenly, 'that you're ahead of us there, Mr Maitland. If the average Russian has a sense of humour, why should Dr Gollnow's possession of the same attribute have any bearing on the case?'

'I feel sure that Sir Charles is going to explain that in due course, my lord.'

'Yes, of course. I don't know how many inhabitants of

the U.S.S.R. are actually party members,' said the witness, not at all put out by the judge's intervention, 'but about those who are it's a very different story. Life is real, life is earnest, and hardly a smile out of the lot of them.'

'So in retrospect this characteristic of Dr Gollnow's makes you feel that his defection isn't altogether a matter for surprise?'

'It's the only thing I can think of.'

'But it's only just occurred to you, now, after my question? Not when you knew him in Moscow?'

'No, certainly not then, but we had quite a long talk you know and he told me —'

'Yes, thank you, Sir Charles. Neither his lordship nor my friend for the prosecution will be very pleased with me if I allow you to repeat that. I'm grateful for your help, I'm sure we must all be grateful for your help,' he added, and exchanged a final smile with the witness before Sir Charles stood down.

The next witness to be called was Dr Boris Gollnow, and it took some time to produce him. 'Goodness knows where they've got him stashed away,' said Maitland to Stringer and encountered a look from Bruce Halloran — who could not possibly have heard what he had said — which could only be described as darkly suspicious. But when Stringer made some light-hearted reply he found himself ignored, and realised that his leader was waiting with some anxiety for the witness's appearance. He was in fact on his feet almost before the Russian was in the witness-box. 'My lord!'

'Yes, Mr Maitland?' If the judge was surprised by the interruption before a single question had been asked, his courteous tone gave no indication of the fact.

'May I make a request of the court?'

'I see no reason why you should not do so. You realise, of course, that this is not to say it will be granted.'

'No, your lordship. It is really a very simple request,'

Antony went on, 'and one to which I'm sure my learned friend, Mr Halloran, can have no objection. Dr Gollnow is a very important witness, and as he is being called so early in the proceedings it may be that some matters arise during later testimony about which I may wish to question him. May I be assured that he will be recalled for further cross-examination if I request it?'

'I see no real objection to that,' Carruthers said slowly. 'What have you to say to it, Mr Halloran?'

'It seems on the face of it a reasonable request, my lord,' said Halloran, succeeding in making it sound as though reason was the last thing he would have expected from the defence. 'Particularly as Mr Maitland has taken over the matter at very short notice and may not be fully cognisant —'

'I'm cognisant of the facts,' Antony was stung into replying. 'I was referring to matters which might emerge in cross-examination.'

'I have no objection, my lord,' said Halloran magnanimously.

'Provided, of course, that the witness is excluded from the court in the meantime,' Carruthers added. 'But perhaps, in the circumstances, that was the intention in any event.'

'It was, my lord. Dr Gollnow is being guarded for his own protection,' Halloran told him. 'He was waiting in a room apart from the other witnesses, and there is no reason why he can't return there.'

'Very well, let that be done. You yourself, doctor,' he added considerately to the witness, 'have no objection to this course, I hope.'

'No objection, my lord.' His English was stiffly correct, but with little or no trace of accent. Though, as far as appearance went, Maitland thought he would have known him anywhere for a Russian; it was odd how these tribal resemblances persisted. It was only later that it occurred to him that he had in mind a very circumscribed area in what was a very large country.

Before the Russian's evidence could begin there was some little discussion as to whether he should give his testimony on oath or merely affirm it. 'As a party member, doctor —' said Halloran carefully.

'Officially, of course, all these years an atheist,' said Gollnow. 'But I assure you it has been a matter of expediency with me, not of principle. I should prefer to swear on a Christian bible to the truth of what I am saying, if that is your custom.'

Not unnaturally, some discussion followed. When it became obvious that the witness meant what he said an Orthodox text was suggested, but this proved elusive so a compromise was finally made with the Douai version. As Halloran got up to begin his questioning his opponent was beginning a sketch on the back of his brief depicting the witness ('Not too bad for a likeness either,' said Stringer when it was shown to him later) almost entirely in a series of squares.

The witness had been looking around the court with interest and perhaps with a little anxiety. Halloran's voice now recalled his attention. 'Will you give us your name, sir?'

'Boris Gollnow.'

'I think we must add to that,' said Halloran, 'of no fixed address.'

The Russian smiled. 'My address at the moment is fixed by my good friends who are taking care of me until my status is decided.'

'May I clarify the form we should use when speaking to you?'

'For myself I do not care. My higher education at Moscow University was technical, you understand. I am a physicist, and I know that in this country only physicians are addressed as doctor. However in my country I have had friends from the United States as well as from England, and

31

it was their custom to speak to me in that way.'

'Then let us follow their example. It was merely the nature of your studies that I wished to get quite clear in the minds of the jury. Now perhaps you will tell us, doctor, a little about the events that led up to your visit to Sir Charles Daniell.'

'Willingly. Since coming to this country I have become more and more disillusioned with the ways of my party. It is difficult to explain, and I think perhaps that no-one who has not been through the whole education system in Russia could quite understand. I am as a young man quite confident of our rightness, but then here it is so different.'

'Yet you have been in this country for four years.'

'Yes, but at first I performed my duties without question. I'm not merely a diplomatic member of the Embassy, you know that, sir. I am a member of the K.G.B., a specialist from Directorate T. And I am here for the express purpose of gathering information which may be of use to my country.'

'And when did you first begin to doubt the — shall we say the rightness of what you were doing?'

'Not immediately. Certainly not immediately. And then there was much soul-searching. Is that the right expression? And perhaps for a year now there has been much disturbance in my mind, yet I have continued a good servant of the party. I have no children, no close relatives, but my wife was still in Russia.'

'I see. You say . . . she was?'

'She died at the end of last year.'

'I am very sorry. So after some further thought —'

'I went to see Sir Charles. I thought it would be easier to talk to him than to someone quite unknown to me, though I know, of course, a good deal about the organisation of such things in this country. And I am right, my friend is sympathetic and knows just what should be done.'

'Will you tell us, then, exactly what you told him?'

'Why, that I wish for political asylum.'

'That we understand. There were other things, however.'

'Many things.'

'Perhaps I should specify that we are now considering your dealings with Dennis Nesbit and John Ryder.'

'Yes, and that was a strange thing. It is my business you understand to search out those who are willing, for gain or for their ideals, to be of help to us. But in this case the approach was made to me.'

'By whom, doctor?'

'By John Ryder.'

'Did you come to know him well?'

'Oh yes, during two years I have met Mr Nesbit regularly at Mr Ryder's flat.'

'Do you recognise him, here in the court?'

Gollnow's eyes went to the man in the dock. 'I recognise that man,' he said.

'Then perhaps we may go back to your talk with Sir Charles Daniell.'

'There were names I could give him of people who had co-operated with me in the past. But you are not interested in them, only in this more recent association. I have told you that in the main I have been the one to make an approach, to satisfy myself, of course, that a proper frame of mind existed in the person I was about to have dealings with. In this instance the contact was initiated by John Ryder.'

'How did that come about?'

'On occasion I dine alone at a small restaurant near the Embassy. I think, perhaps, I need not enlarge upon the reasons for this. One evening Ryder came to my table, apologised very civilly for disturbing me, and asked if he might join me as he had something to communicate. I realised then that I had several times seen him dining there in company with a lady, but this evening he was alone. And, of course, I agreed to talk to him, though keeping always at

33

the back of my mind the possibility that the authorities had found out in some way what I was doing and that this approach might be a trick.'

'Do you remember the date?'

'Yes, it was in December, 1971, which explains my suspicions. Barely three months after so many of my colleagues had been expelled from this country.'

'But he managed to dispel your fears.'

'Yes. I think you will realise that in the work I have been doing an ability to judge character is a very essential thing. You may think it odd that I should come to trust a man who was willing to betray his country, but I have seen too many men, especially young men, in the grip of an ideal, willing to treat Communism as we of the party do — as I myself once did — almost as a religion. This was how that man regarded it, and I soon became convinced of the truth of what he was telling me.'

'The question remains how did he know you were a suitable person to approach?'

'He gave me the name of one of my former colleagues, who had left England not altogether willingly the previous September. This man had been in touch with him, and when he knew that it was inevitable that he should leave had given him my name. Of course I checked all this with him later.'

'But that was three months previously.'

'Ryder said he had been waiting to see whether I should be sent from the country too.'

'And then?'

'He said that, willing as he would be to do so, he himself had no information to communicate that would be useful to me. But his position as a contracts administrator with Wycherley's, who I understand are a very large firm of defence contractors, put him in touch with all sorts of people. It was then that he mentioned Dennis Nesbit, who worked at the Admiralty Underwater Weapons

Establishment.'

'And after that?'

'I checked his story, as I told you. My colleague was able to assure me of his good faith as far as he had been able to establish it. Ryder had said that his flat in Bloomsbury would be a suitable place for meetings. He himself worked at the firm's main plant in Wolverhampton but was in the habit of spending one week in three at the London office. As his wife preferred living in town, that was where he made his home. I met Dennis Nesbit there three weeks later, and regularly at three-week intervals after that.'

'I think there is no reason to go into precise details of the information he gave you, as I imagine that it was classified material.'

'It would not have been of interest to me otherwise,' Gollnow agreed.

'But perhaps you will tell us whether or not the information was useful to you.'

'Potentially useful to my country, certainly. He gave me details about a particular project, though as the work is still in an experimental stage I have no real idea whether the basic premise is sound or not.'

'Was John Ryder present at these meetings?'

'Invariably. Nesbit would bring papers, drawings, and there was an excellent copying-machine in the room Mr Ryder used as his study. He would make copies for me to take away with me, and Mr Nesbit could take the originals back to their place in his files and no one the wiser.'

'And Mrs Ryder? The woman you knew as Mrs Ryder.'

'Our business together did not take very long. We would join her afterwards for coffee and a drink. She was kind enough to buy vodka for me, though not a very good brand.'

And that effectively was the end of Halloran's direct examination of the witness. There were, of course, some points he wished to emphasise, and it was actually a half hour later before Maitland rose to cross-examine. After Halloran's careful explanation of the law there wasn't much point in stressing the fact that John Ryder had had no direct communications to make to the Russians, but he tried a question or two on those lines first and got satisfactory answers, though how far they impressed the jury was another matter. After that something prompted him to add, 'I gather that Mrs Ryder, the woman who was living with John Ryder as his wife, knew your nationality.'

'Certainly she did.'

'Do you know what explanation had been given to her for your visits?'

Halloran seemed about to get up, but subsided again. 'She treated me as she might have done any other friend of her husband's,' said Dr Gollnow.

'Did she know, for instance, that you were attached to the Embassy?'

This time Bruce Halloran did get up. 'My lord, may I ask my learned friend whether he wishes to discredit Miss Paull?'

'Is that your intention, Mr Maitland?'

'I'm afraid, my lord, that is a question that I can't answer at this stage of the proceedings.'

'Then I shall disallow the question. Dr Gollnow can't answer of his own knowledge, and you will have the opportunity of putting it to the lady yourself later on.'

'If you lordship pleases. Will you tell us, Dr Gollnow, what occurred when you met my client after his arrest. Did you pick him out from among other men, or was it rather a confrontation?'

'As his wife had already identified him —'

'I should like an answer to my question.'

'There was no — no line-up, I believe you call it.'

'In other words, when you first saw my client you already knew you were being taken to see a man called John Ryder?'

'When I first saw him after his arrest,' Gollnow corrected him placidly.

'I see. Then I have just one more question for you, doctor. There was something else that you told Sir Charles, wasn't there?'

'I said . . . many things.'

This time the judge spoke before Halloran could do so. 'Mr Maitland, enough has been said to show the seriousness of the disclosures made to this witness. Unless the defence is prepared to prove that they were not of a classified nature —'

'The defence will produce no arguments on that score.'

'Then no further details are necessary.'

'That wasn't quite what was in my mind, my lord.' But he felt Derek's hand on his sleeve and recognised the touch as a warning. Too many questions could be as dangerous as too few. 'I have nothing more to ask the witness,' he added and sat down rather abruptly.

It was at this point, while Dr Gollnow was being conducted from the court to whatever secure hiding-place the S.I.S. had found for him, that Maitland twisted round to speak to Geoffrey Horton, sitting behind him. 'I want to talk to Ryder tonight before they take him away,' he said. 'Can you arrange that, Geoffrey?'

Geoffrey was perhaps past being surprised at any request his mercurial friend might make of him. 'Yes, if you like,' he said. 'What about you, Derek, will you sit in on the discussion?'

'Would there be any point? I admit', said Stringer, 'I don't quite see why you should change your mind about that, Antony.'

But Maitland's attention had already drifted back to the trial and to the man who was just stepping into the witness-box. 'I'd like to hear what he has to say for himself,' he replied, and suppressed a smile at Geoffrey's muttered comment. 'I knew it was too much to expect that you'd read all your brief.'

The witness was sworn in merely as Mr K. though Maitland recognised him as someone he had met when they were both very young, and knew that the recognition was mutual when he caught the other man's eye. Mr K. was describing how he and a colleague, Y, had answered Sir Charles Daniell's summons, their introduction to Dr Gollnow (the implication was they had known of him quite well already) and the action they had taken following his disclosures. No mention was made of anything except the case in hand, and Maitland, during this merely corroboratory part of the evidence, amused himself by imagining what sort of a hornet's nest must have been stirred up at the S.I.S. headquarters when the full scope of the defector's revelations became known.

'The first thing, naturally, was to arrange for Dr Gollnow's safety,' Mr K. was saying, a statement quite true in its way but also covering a multitude of activity mainly directed towards finding out whether the Russian was in fact sincere. 'After that my colleague and I arranged to see Mr Dennis Nesbit. That was not until the following day, the eleventh of February.'

'One moment.' Halloran turned towards the judge. 'My lord, at this point I must ask the court's indulgence, and that of my friend Mr Maitland too. Mr Nesbit is dead and cannot be called as a witness, and I submit that in the circumstances what he told this gentleman should be admitted in evidence, and also a statement he made subsequently in writing, a suicide note in fact, which I think you will agree should come under the definition of a dying declaration.'

'Yes, Mr Halloran, I can see no objection to that. Mr Maitland?'

'The defence has no objection, your lordship.' Seeing the judge's rather grim smile he added to himself, 'and a fat lot of good it would have done if we had,' but the request was fair enough and he knew it.

'Thank you, my lord.' Bruce Halloran's gratitude sounded just as sincere as if he had never been in any doubt of the answer to his submission. 'Now, sir,' — he turned back to Mr K. — 'we can hear the account of your talk with Mr Nesbit without any scruples as to its being hearsay evidence.'

Mr K needed no further prompting. 'It was on a Monday morning that we saw him at his office. He expressed surprise when we identified ourselves, so I asked him point-blank to tell us about his relationship with Dr Gollnow. He repeated the name several times in a rather bewildered way, and then added, "He sounds like a Russian." I said, "I think you know every well that he is a Russian, and that he is ostensibly attached to the Embassy, though his duties here have been far from diplomatic." Mr Nesbit continued to insist that he didn't know anybody by that name, that he had no Russians among his friends or even among his acquaintances. And went on to say, rather naïvely, that if I meant the man was a spy he was quite sure his word (Nesbit's) would be taken before this other man's. Both my colleague and I continued to question him on these lines for some time, but when it became obvious that he was going to make no admission I thought it best to give him a full account of our talk with Dr Gollnow.

'I made this as circumstantial as I could, but when I reached the point that the doctor was asking for political asylum he said immediately, "Oh, that's it then, he wants to buy his way in. And somehow he's hit on my name. There's no end to the things these chaps can find out." So we went on to tell him that we had reason to believe the meetings had taken place at Brinkley Court, at the home of a Mr John Ryder. He hesitated for a moment and then said, "Of course I know John. I can't deny either that I've been to Brinkley Court on occasion to see him and his wife. But why you should suppose there's a matter of espionage mixed up in all this —"

'I interrupted him at this point to explain the nature of

the charges that might be made against him if Dr Gollnow's statement was confirmed, in consequence of the provisions of the Official Secrets Act, but as it seemed important to take steps to obtain that confirmation before we went any further, after a few more routine questions we left. I think he must have realised that once we had visited Ryder's flat —'

'Just one moment, sir. I think perhaps we had better take your actions in order. The next thing I believe was the visit to the flat at Brinkley Court.'

'Yes, indeed it was. Mrs Ryder let us in, and though, of course, she was worried and upset by our visit she made no difficulty about our searching the place. Everything was exactly as Dr Gollnow had told us. We impounded the papers, which were of a highly secret nature, and then asked Mrs Ryder when her husband would be in.'

'I think, my lord, that we should at this point make it clear that the Mrs Ryder to whom this witness is referring is in fact Miss Winifred Paull, though she went through a form of marriage with John Ryder in October, 1971. In fact John Ryder had been married to another woman six months before.'

'Yes, Mr Halloran, I think we're quite clear about that,' Carruthers told him. 'I gather', he added to the witness, 'that you refer to the lady in that way because that was how she introduced herself to you.'

'Yes, my lord, it was. In answer to my question she told me that it wasn't her husband's week for being at home, at present he worked at the Wolverhampton plant of Wycherley's which is also the firm's head office, though he was hoping for a transfer to London soon. That, she said, was why they had made their home there, as they both preferred town living. As a matter of fact John Ryder was arrested at Wolverhampton, where he was found to have another home and another wife. Perhaps I should mention at this point that, as he protested vigorously that it was a

40

case of mistaken identity, we arranged to have him identified both by Dr Gollnow and by the other Mrs Ryder, or Miss Paull if that is more correct. Neither of them showed any hesitation in their recognition of him. In addition it would perhaps be relevant to mention here that his passport was found in a drawer of the desk in the room at Number 301 which seemed to have been furnished as a study.'

'But the identification came later.'

'Yes, it did. Several days later in the case of Dr Gollnow.'

'So we may get back to Mr Nesbit. You didn't ask him also to identify that the Wolverhampton John Ryder was the same one as the London one?'

'It was much too late for that. I'm sorry to have got ahead of my story, since you set so much stock on the chronological order. The very same day that we interviewed Mr Nesbit, he went out at lunchtime, told one of the local chemists that he was suffering badly from insomnia and needed something as strong as possible without a prescription to help him overcome it. He then went back to his office, took the entire bottle of pills, told his secretary that he would be working on important papers and must on no account be disturbed, and was in a deep coma by the time he was discovered. He was, of course, rushed to hospital, but it was too late to save him.'

'He did, however, leave a note explaining his actions?'

'Yes, he did.'

'I shall be placing this letter into evidence, my lord,' Halloran put in. 'It is the original, but I believe the witness has a copy in his possession.'

'Then by all means let him read it,' said the judge when the formalities had been complied with and the document had been duly marked as an exhibit.

Mr K. had assumed a gigantic pair of spectacles. 'This is a photocopy of the original,' he explained. 'The handwriting is a little erratic, I am told no more so than Mr Nesbit's generally was. I mention the fact only because it

41

may make my reading a little hesitant.'

'I should add, my lord,' said Halloran, 'that we shall be calling a handwriting expert to verify the fact that the letter was written by Dennis Nesbit. And his secretary to attest that when she found him at five o'clock that afternoon the letter was lying on his blotting-pad under him, where he had fallen across the desk.'

'Thank you, Mr Halloran. You may proceed,' Carruthers added kindly to the witness.

'Thank you, my lord. It is in fact very brief, and starts without any greeting, though it is dated.'

'The eleventh of February, 1974?' Halloran asked.

'Yes. As I said, it starts abruptly: *I have thought about what happened this morning, and it is obvious that they know everything. Obvious, too, that with Gollnow in their hands my usefulness to his countrymen is over, even if I thought there was any possibility of my leaving England. Strangely, now it comes to the point, I find I do not wish to do so. All these years, ever since John Ryder approached me, I have been telling myself that what I was doing was a matter of principle, now I am very much afraid it was no more than a desire for the good things of life, for the things I could give to and share with my wife. To you, my dear Elsie, I leave my love and my sorrow for the position I am putting you in. John was very persuasive. Without his very specious arguments I do not think I should ever have fallen into this error.* That is all,' said Mr K. looking up and removing his spectacles. 'Except, of course, for the signature, which as counsel has said will be attested to by an expert.'

All this had taken time but all the same Maitland was a little surprised when Mr Justice Carruthers, perhaps from some hitherto unsuspected sense of drama, chose this moment to adjourn for the day.

III

As soon as the judge had retired Geoffrey left them, to return in a surprisingly short time to say that he had arranged for a room to be at their disposal so that they could interview their client. On the whole Antony was glad that Derek had decided not to sit in on the talk. In fact he'd have been glad enough, as Geoffrey knew only too well, if etiquette hadn't demanded that the solicitor accompany him. For getting at the truth the fewer distractions there were for the witness the better, and even one extra person present might make a difference. Not that he was surprised by Stringer's decision. His colleague was one of those fortunate people who are apt to see things in black and white, and to whom their own duty is always quite clear cut.

The room selected for the interview was as dismal as such places are apt to be. John Ryder had a wary look as he came in and listened to Geoffrey's introduction of his new counsel. He was frowning slightly as he turned to face Maitland. 'I'm grateful to you for taking over my case on such short notice,' he said formally. He looked younger than he had seemed from the dock, and the note of caution was perhaps not characteristic. Maitland felt that behind it there was a faint trace of hostility, which it would be better for both of their sakes to bring out into the open.

'All the same —?' he said on a note of inquiry.

'I had several talks with Mr O'Brien.'

'Mr Maitland took over at very short notice,' said Geoffrey in a hurry. 'It hasn't —' He stopped when Antony held up his hand.

'You're quite right, Mr Ryder,' he said. 'I thought this was a matter that could be dealt with quite well merely from the study of my brief. But you're quite right too that we should have a talk. Won't you sit down, then we can get on with it?'

'Very well.' That was still said grudgingly, but he seated himself without further comment and looked expectantly from one to the other of the two lawyers. 'What do you want to know?'

'Everything,' said Maitland simply.

Unexpectedly, Ryder smiled. 'That's a tall order,' he said.

'You asked me, and I told you. I know you're pleading Not Guilty,' he added rather as though he were making a concession.

'It's perfectly true,' said Ryder quickly.

'Let's go on from there then. How long had you known Dennis Nesbit?'

'I never met him.'

'And Dr Gollnow?'

'How would I get to know a chap like that? Mr Horton must have told you . . . but if you won't believe a word I say, what's the use?'

'Tell me from the beginning, then. The beginning as far as you are concerned.'

'That was when those two men came to my office exactly four weeks ago today. The gentleman who was giving evidence just now, and a colleague of his, this Mr Y. he spoke about. They were able to convince me that they were who they said they were, at least as far as their job was concerned. But I still don't know their real names,' he added, as though that contributed the final straw to his resentment.

'Your office at Wycherley's is in Wolverhampton?'

'Yes. I'd been in London the week before, so now I was home, I thought, for two weeks.'

'Home?'

'You're thinking about this nonsense of there being two Mrs Ryders. Honestly, I don't understand that, Mr Maitland.' Now he sounded merely bewildered.

44

'We'll come to that in a moment. Just take things in order.'

'Well, they asked me to confirm who I was, and of course they could see I worked at Wycherley's, so they asked me then whether my duties didn't take me rather frequently to London. I said yes they did, one week in three on average, and they said — it was this chap who was giving evidence today who did most of the talking — that when I was in London I lived at Brinkley Court, didn't I? Naturally I said yes to that too. And that was the first time I realised there must have been some sort of muddle, because they said, at Number 301? and I said, no, at Number 417. That's my sister's place.'

'Just pretend I haven't heard any of this before, Mr Ryder.'

'My sister Edwina is married to a man called Henry Mason, who is a civil engineer. They're often abroad for months at a time. Of course when they're home I use their spare room, but when they're away as they are at the moment — in South America as it happens — I use it just the same.'

'Have you any friends among your neighbours there?'

'I see people in the lift sometimes whom I know by sight, though I don't know their names and I don't suppose they know mine. You see I'm just there for five nights, and on the Sunday I arrive fairly late, and on Thursday evening I'm cleaning up after myself.'

'Ready for the next time?'

'Yes, that's part of it. But the thing is you never know when you'll see Henry. That's not a criticism, he's an awfully good chap, but if he decided he wanted a week in London he'd wangle it somehow or other. And Edwina, who is a little older than I am, is inclined to be critical if everything isn't just so. Perhaps that's the way with sisters, I don't know. Anyway, I always make sure things are exactly as they should be, just in case.'

'I see. Now I understand, Mr Ryder, that in the entrance to the block of flats there's a board with the names of tenants, and a bell beside each one for visitors to ring to be admitted to the building. Beside Number 301 are the names *Mr and Mrs John Ryder*. Have you ever noticed that and wondered about the coincidence?'

'I've never had occasion to consult the list at all, barely glanced at it even. I have my own keys to both doors, and even when I know Edwina and Henry are at home I let myself in downstairs without bothering them.'

'It sometimes happens that one notices one's own name where a stranger's might pass one by.'

'Well, it didn't happen in this case. I don't think the printing is very large as a matter of fact. I've noticed people putting on their glasses to peer at the list.'

Maitland glanced at Geoffrey who nodded his confirmation. 'How long have your sister and her husband been away on this occasion?'

'Simply ages. That's why I thought Henry would give way sooner or later to the impulse to come back to town, even if only for a brief visit.'

'I'm afraid ''ages'' won't do for the court, Mr Ryder.'

'Well, it depends whether you mean since the job started or since the last time they came home for a brief visit.'

'I'd like the answer to both of those questions.'

'I think they first went out almost exactly two and a half years ago. It was September, I remember — that would make in 1971, wouldn't it? It was a trouble-shooting job you see, Henry says they're much the most difficult. But they have been home since, for Christmas, a year ago, or fifteen months if you want to be exact. They spent the time with us in Wolverhampton. That's why I've been thinking they were just about due for another break.'

'Didn't they visit the flat at all on that occasion?'

'Oh yes, it was my week up here after the holiday, so we all came up together and had a week in London. I saw them off before I went back home.'

'When you say all, Mr Ryder, do you mean Mrs Caroline Ryder as well?'

'No, unfortunately, Carol hadn't any time owing to her just then and couldn't get away from her job.'

'Did she never accompany you to London?'

'As a matter of fact, no. Spending so much time here I didn't want to come back when we were on holiday, and Carol prefers the country anyway. We usually took a touring holiday, which was something we both enjoyed.'

'You didn't know Dennis Nesbit, you don't know Dr Gollnow. That brings us to the questions of these two marriages, doesn't it?'

'I married Carol, three years ago in St Mark's Church in Bloxwich, and that's it as far as I'm concerned. I never saw this other woman before.'

'And yet she identified you when you were brought back to London?'

'Yes, she did, and I don't understand it. And you know, Mr Maitland, I'm not really surprised they believed her, she was utterly convincing. They took me to Brinkley Court, and there was no way she could have known . . . yet she spoke to me as familiarly as if we had been man and wife for years and she asked what I'd been up to because they'd been searching the flat, you see — her flat, Number 301. And I remember her saying, "He's my husband . . . well that's what I thought." And that was really when it all began to be a complete nightmare, because I'd been so sure, you see, they'd just mistaken me for another man with the same name. John Ryder isn't exactly uncommon so I was certain as soon as I met the supposed Mrs Ryder everything would be cleared up.'

'Mr K. mentioned the date of the marriage as October, 1971. What was the exact date, Geoffrey?'

'The fifth.'

'Had you any records to tell whether that was one of the

47

weeks you'd been in London?'

'I had and it was. Worse than that,' he added, his eyes on Maitland's face as though every change of expression there were life and death to him, 'it was one of the few occasions I stayed over till Saturday, and now this blasted woman says we had to wait two weeks for our honeymoon. Business reasons, she says. And she had all the details of my job off pat. And she said — well you heard what was said in court — that I was hoping for a transfer, and so we decided to set up housekeeping in London anyway.'

'Disconcerting,' said Maitland rather tonelessly. 'And then you were confronted with Dr Gollnow?'

'Yes, and of course that was the last straw, because I'd thought he at least would say that he's never seen me before, even if she was stark, staring mad.'

'Were there any further identifications?'

'Don't you think those were enough?'

'I'm afraid so. All the same I should like an answer to my question,' said Antony rather sharply. He felt Geoffrey's eyes on him and added more gently, 'This supposed wedding, for instance. Where did it take place?'

'Some registry office, they said. I was put in a line-up, and they produced the registrar and the two witnesses, who turned out to be charwomen in the building. They all saw so many people all the time, they just couldn't say. Not even that I was familiar. And the signature in the register was just a scrawl that could have meant anything. Only I know what they'll say about that, it was a bigamous marriage so I didn't want to sign my usual way, which is quite legible actually.'

'Yes, I'm afraid that's exactly what they will say. Can we get back now to the marriage you admit to, the one in Bloxwich?'

'I'm not denying that.'

'No, I know. All the same the — may I call her the second Mrs Ryder — describes a rather strange domestic

48

arrangement, with you away two weeks out of three. The converse is almost as odd.'

'I don't really want to talk about that.' A look of stubborness seemed to settle on the prisoner's face.

'Considering the circumstances, Mr Ryder —'

'Yes, I know! My likes and dislikes don't come into the matter,' said Ryder bitterly. 'If you must know, this two weeks at head office and one week in London arrangement has been going on for almost five years, and Carol knew all about it before we were married.'

'That was three years ago you say?'

'Yes, and that *can* be proved, because it wasn't a hole-in-the-wall affair, we knew everyone there. So whatever happens Carol won't have that to reproach me with, even if she believes I'm a bigamist she'll know she was really my wife.'

'Just a minute, Mr Ryder.' It wasn't often Geoffrey interrupted when Maitland was in full flight with a witness, but this time he did so quite firmly. 'I told you I've seen Mrs Ryder, she's quite firmly convinced of your innocence.'

'Yes, she'd say so, she's a faithful little thing. But even if she was telling the truth when you saw her, Mr Horton, do you think she'll still believe me by the time the court's finished. By the time all the evidence is in. I don't know what's happening to us, but the way one thing after another comes up I'm beginning to feel as if the end's inevitable.'

'I just don't think you should discount Mrs Ryder's trust in you,' Geoffrey told him stubbornly.

'She's so —' He broke off there and thought for a moment. 'Vulnerable,' he said at last. 'You know, Mr Maitland, she's expecting a baby, and ever since she became pregnant she's been . . . different.'

'Tell me,' Antony invited.

'You wanted to know about the arrangement that meant my being away so much. We've been living in a rented

49

cottage on the outskirts of the town, not big enough to raise a family in, but we both want children . . . wanted children I should say. So Carol went on with her job, even though that meant I had to leave her behind when I went to London. If we hadn't been trying to save every penny for the down payment on a house it wouldn't have been too expensive her coming with me, especially as we could both have stayed at my sister's.'

'How long has she been pregnant?'

'About five months. Of course we didn't know straight away, but I'd already noticed the difference in her. She seemed to get edgy about the arrangement, about my being away, even though she tried very hard not to show it. The last time I saw her —'

'The last time you saw her,' Maitland prompted, when his client seemed disinclined to continue.

'We nearly quarrelled. That's why it was just hell not being able to see her again. Oh I know what you say, Mr Horton, and I'm grateful to you for trying to put the best complexion on things. Any other time I might believe you, but —'

'You were telling us about the last time you saw your wife,' said Antony. And all at once John Ryder, that unwilling witness, was speaking as though the words couldn't come fast enough.

'She said all her friends told her they didn't know how she put up with it,' he said, 'and she meant my being away so much. She gave me half a smile as she said it, as though to say I needn't take her seriously unless I wanted to, but there'd been too much of that, I knew she meant it underneath. But then — ' only too obviously he was back in the past, his dreary surroundings and the men who were questioning him completely forgotten — 'she almost apologised, and said something about it being just these last few months that she'd felt like that. Only she just couldn't leave the subject alone. She said, ''I know where you go of

50

course, but I don't know what you're doing.'' And I was fool enough to remind her that she knew how it would be when we got married.'

'Neither comforting nor conciliatory,' Maitland agreed, nodding. 'But it was hardly the end of the world.'

'I was annoyed, you see, because I didn't want to go any more than she wanted me to. But there's a funny little wriggle of her shoulder she gives, not quite a shrug, and she did that as she moved away from me, and it was so familiar and so expressive of what she was feeling that I couldn't help laughing in spite of being annoyed. That made her really angry. She said she expected I really liked the trips, or surely I could arrange for somebody else to go for once.'

'Could you?'

'Not really, you see I knew the ropes. Anyone else from the department would have spent the whole week finding out what was supposed to be done. But it was no use explaining that, she knew it perfectly well already. So I just told her if I had much more of it I'd beat her, which she knew was a lie, and that made her smile, though rather shakily, and she looked down quite complacently at the perfectly dreadful, shapeless dress she was wearing and said, "Surely not, Mr Ryder? The mother of your children!" I said I hoped that wasn't a tactful way of telling me the doctor said it was twins, but my suitcase was packed by that time — did I tell you this was going on in the bedroom? — and there wasn't time for any more or I'd have missed my train.'

It was one of Sir Nicholas's favourite dicta that one should never become emotionally involved in a client's affairs. Antony wondered briefly how often he had ignored that advice, but this was one occasion when he had every intention of taking it. 'So your story is that you're happily married to your wife, Caroline, and had no need for any — shall we say diversions? — on your trips to London.'

'That's my story and it happens to be true. Look here, if I

51

wanted to carry on with anyone I wouldn't have needed to have married them.'

'In the ordinary way, no. I'm afraid what my friend Mr Halloran will say is that you married this girl, Winifred Paull, to keep her mouth shut; or rather, as she professes to know nothing of what was going on, to prevent her from asking awkward questions. That's quite a plausible answer to your objection, Mr Ryder.'

'There's a plausable answer to everything I say as far as I can see.'

'Let's try again then. The second flat at Brinkley Court, Number 301, was taken by Mrs Ryder — my use of that name implies neither belief nor disbelief in your statement, Mr Ryder — during the period when she was waiting for her honeymoon to begin. At the same time she opened a bank account, out of which the rent was paid each month, and out of which she drew living expenses as necessary, on a fairly lavish scale. All the deposits — yes I know you gave me a list of them, Geoffrey, and I've got it somewhere but I can't remember the amounts now — all the deposits were made in cash. They were quite considerable —'

'But Caroline and I didn't have a penny to spare. Her salary went straight into a deposit account, and that can be proved too.'

'I'm afraid there's an answer to that as well, Mr Ryder, as I am sure Mr Horton has pointed out to you already. That the London money was paid to you by a foreign government for services rendered.'

'But I told you . . . yes, I know by now a simple denial is no use. But if the account is in this other woman's name, this Winifred Paull who calls herself Mrs Ryder, how would it benefit me?'

'It's very difficult to prove a negative. We can assure the court that you have no other bank account in your own or in an assumed name, but there's no earthly way we can prove it.'

'And there's another thing, nobody's spoken about fingerprints but if they examined Number 301 as carefully as I suppose they did, how do they explain there aren't any of mine there? Because there aren't, there can't be, I've never been in the place.'

'Your . . . I'm sorry, Miss Paull says she cleaned the place after you left on the Friday, just as you say you cleaned up your sister's flat very thoroughly on Thursday night.'

'I've explained why I did that.'

'Yes I know, but one story is as likely as another. This girl would say, I'm sure — it's implicit in her evidence — that she's very much in love with you, and what better cure for loneliness is there than a little housework?'

'It just isn't true! That I was ever there, I mean.'

'Let's leave it for the moment. That particular point looks very like a stalemate. You mentioned at one point, Mr Ryder, that you generally arrived late on Sunday evening when you came to Brinkley Court, and spent Thursday evenings cleaning up. By the way, did that include clearing out the refrigerator and so forth?'

'Yes, it did. Edwina had a particular horror of odd bits of food left about. I made sure that the ice-trays were filled, of course, but I got pretty well used to judging exactly how much food I'd need for the few mornings I'd be there.'

'You only ate breakfast at the flat?'

'That's right.'

'That brings us to the question of what you did with your other three evenings. You say you knew none of your neighbours at Brinkley Court.'

'No, and of course I wish now that I had done. They'd have been able to say where I was living, I mean which flat was mine. But over the years I'd got pretty friendly with the three marketing types who were in the London office. I suppose one of them invited me to dinner at his home every other time I was down here, and the other weeks I'd be

53

repaying their hospitality. I'm not saying there was any hard and fast rule about that, perhaps one evening in each of the weeks I spent here would be in their company.'

'And the other two evenings?'

'I'm not much of a cook, I prefer to eat out.'

'I'm sure Mr Horton has gone into this, but there was nothing — am I wronging you, Geoffrey? — in the documents that accompanied my brief.'

'I'm quite sure I mentioned it somewhere,' said Horton, and did not add, as he might well have done, that it was far more likely that Maitland had missed the reference than that he had omitted it. 'But perhaps you'd like to hear Mr Ryder's answer for yourself.'

'How well you know me. What about it, Mr Ryder?'

'Those evenings I was at a loose end, I didn't just stick to the little place round the corner or anything like that. In any case, my expenses weren't too large with having free lodging at my sister's — I'm on a fixed allowance from the firm, but I never could persuade her to accept a penny of it — so I felt I could spread myself a little and eat at a different place most nights. That's another thing I can't prove, but it's the way it was.'

'That I can understand. And when you were entertaining these colleagues of yours?'

'The same thing applied.'

'You won't be happy about all this,' said Geoffrey in a resigned tone. 'I've had inquiries made at every single one of the restaurants that Mr Ryder says he visited during the last six months, and not one of them remember him, except a place called Ricardo's, where he says he entertained more than once. I didn't think it was worth going back further than that.'

'No, I don't think so either. I was forgetting though, you were talking about the lack of fingerprints at Number 301, Mr Ryder. You'll remember, though, that your passport was found there. And some clothes that the girl said

54

belonged to you.'

'The passport is certainly mine, but I didn't even know it was missing.'

'When had you last seen it?'

'I haven't had occasion to go abroad for some time. Eighteen months or so, I should say. I always had it in my briefcase with me, in case something came up while I was in London, but it's not the kind of thing you think about when you don't need it.'

'Did you leave it in the flat?'

'It wouldn't be much use there. No, I took it to the office each day, there'd be papers I needed.'

'But you still didn't notice —'

'I told you . . . no!'

'And the clothes?'

'I'd never seen them before.'

'They fitted, however?'

'Oh yes, they fitted. And they were the kind of thing I might wear too. And if you're going to comment next on the fact that there wasn't much of mine at Number 417, you're quite right. Shirts and socks and underwear and pyjamas had to go back home to be washed, so I just took enough with me for the week, and it was quite easy to pack the other things I needed at the same time.'

'All right then, we'll leave that point. Tell me about these three colleagues of yours,' Maitland invited.

'You mean the three men at the London office? What interest can they be to you?'

'I'm interested,' said Maitland patiently, 'because the prosecution are calling all of them as witnesses. And the wives of two of them,' he added. The truth so far as it went at least, he congratulated himself.

'Well . . . it's difficult to know where to begin.'

'Start with the top man then and work your way down. Marketing types I think you said? In my innocence I thought your sort of thing sold itself.'

'Another company might call them Advance Projects. Their job is to come up with new ideas, and the office is in London to make the ministry people easily available to them when they do. Also, of course, there's the question of selling abroad. That can be handled better from here.'

'Your own job?'

'Oh, that concerns projects already in progress. There again, somebody has to be in touch part of the time with the powers that be, and people are much more leery than they used to be about the inviolability of a telephone message.'

'Yes, I can see that would be the case. Back to these three men.'

'The one who runs things is called Donald Walters. I happen to know his age because he mentioned once not long since that he was three years off retirement. He's been with Wycherley's for ever, did his apprenticeship with them, and he seems an exceptionally bright chap. I think he's unlucky not to have got further than he has. Ernest — that's Ernest Braithwaite, I'll come to him in a minute — told me once that he thought it was because Mr Walters was very strong on ideas, but not so hot when it came to applying them. I don't know whether that's right or not, but certainly the present managing director, for instance, was apprenticed at the same time that he was. He's not married so it must be Jane and Edith they're calling, I can't think why.'

'The others then. This Ernest Braithwaite you mentioned.'

'He and William Gibbon are both about my age. Perhaps, on reflection, Ernest may be a little older — he was already with Wycherley's when I joined them. William came along about a year later. And they're both married; Ernest's wife is Jane and William's is Edith.'

'If those two are nearer to you in age, presumably you got to know them better than you did Mr Walters.'

'The answer to that is, yes and no. We'd more in common, certainly, but their habit in general is to go to lunch together early, leaving Mr Walters to go later, alone. So I fell into the habit of joining him when I was in town.'

'And in addition to that you dined together fairly regularly, just the two of you?'

'That's right. I wouldn't be at all surprised to find he thought it a bit of a nuisance, and only asked me out of courtesy.'

'To his home, I think you said.'

'Not in his case, except that we'd usually go straight to his flat from the office, have a drink, and then go to dinner somewhere. Look here, I can't see why on earth anyone should want their evidence. Whether you believe me about my innocence or not, you may believe me when I tell you that I certainly didn't talk to any of them about being in touch with the Russian Embassy or with this chap Gollnow either.'

'Let's go into this a little further and see if anything emerges. For instance, you mentioned returning hospitality. When you did this with Mr Walters, did the same thing apply? Did you go to your sister's flat, and then out for a meal?'

'No, we'd go straight to the restaurant. I usually chose one with a bar so that we could sit quietly for a while before we ordered our meal.'

'Why was that?'

Ryder frowned over the question. 'I find that rather difficult to answer,' he said. 'I suppose it must be that I'm always very conscious of it being Edwina's flat, Edwina and Henry's, of course, so that I never feel truly at home there.'

'With the other two?'

'If you mean did I take Ernest and Jane home or William and Edith, no I didn't. And I suppose for the same reason, though I admit I've never given it much thought.'

'Did you take those four out together, or seperately?'

'Sometimes one, sometimes the other, however it fitted in with their arrangements. I told you there was no hard and fast rule about it.'

'Thank you, Mr Ryder. Now I know Mr Horton has been through your evidence with you, I have your proof here, so I won't worry you any more at the moment. Just one last thing. When you were confronted with the so-called Mrs Ryder, did you recognise her as a fellow-tenant?'

'No, and if I'd ever seen her I think I should have done. She's a rather brassy female.'

Maitland smiled at that and got to his feet. 'Not your type,' he suggested.

'Not at all my type.' Ryder got up too, and stood looking from one to the other of the two lawyers. 'If even one person believed me —' he said, and broke off there and shrugged.

'There are twelve jurors,' said Maitland noncommittally, and wasn't surprised when, after their farewells had been said and they were almost outside the building, Geoffrey turned on him almost accusingly.

'You're beginning to believe him,' he said.

'I'm beginning to wonder,' said Antony slowly. 'And you can't blame me, Geoffrey, because you know perfectly well you've been wondering yourself, at least ever since Caroline Ryder came to see you.'

'She only wanted to help.'

'I'm not accusing her of anything. I wish I could see how she could be useful, but calling her would only serve to rub it well into the jury that Ryder's alleged to have had two wives. The case against him is strong enough without having the more moralistic among the jurors taking a dislike to him for that reason and no other.'

'No, I agree with you about that. And as she is so very obviously in love with him she'd be no use on the subject of character. All the same, Antony, Halloran's only just started calling his witnesses, the damn thing's as near cast iron as makes no matter.'

'How many times have I to tell you that I read my brief,' said Maitland. He caught sight of a cruising taxi and raised

58

his left arm. 'No more tonight, there's a good fellow. We'll get together before court in the morning and talk over the implications of what our client said, and put Derek in the picture at the same time.'

As the cab drew up beside them at that point, Geoffrey had no chance to argue.

IV

It was Tuesday evening, and on Tuesday evenings from time immemorial Sir Nicholas, and now Sir Nicholas and Vera, Lady Harding, had dined with the Maitlands. As his talk with John Ryder had delayed him, it was only to be expected that they would have arrived upstairs before Antony got home, and he took Gibbs's rather pointed and unsympathetic remark about his lateness — again! — as he went through the hall as something far too familiar to waste two thoughts on.

If an unexpected visitor had arrived it was likely that Jenny would come out into the upstairs hall to warn him of what was in store, but on Tuesday evenings he would generally get into the living-room to find her already pouring sherry. He was a little surprised therefore when she came out of the living-room and closed the door carefully behind her. 'Uncle Nick's in the sort of mood when he's all set to demand instant explanations,' she said.

'Is he though? I don't know if I have any particularly good ones on hand at the moment.'

Jenny must have thought he was taking the matter too lightly. 'As he'd say himself, *verbum sap*,' she said seriously.

Antony grinned at her. 'My dearest love, you're wrong about that. If he used the phrase at all, which I doubt, he'd use it in its entirety,' he said. 'Anyway, my conscience is clear . . . well, comparatively clear,' he assured her. 'Come on, love, it's been a long day and I need a drink.'

'And you shall have one.' She preceded him into the living-room. Antony, pausing to close the door, took an instant, as he often did, to savour the moment of homecoming: the big, comfortable, shabby room where so many out-of-court battles had been fought, but which was still a place of refuge because of Jenny's special serenity, with which she seemed to have the gift of endowing her surroundings. She was standing by the writing-desk in the corner with her back to him, dealing with his request as though the exact amount she transfered from decanter to glass was a matter of life and death.

Near her in the wing chair to the right of the hearth Sir Nicholas was stretched out very much at his ease, sipping occasionally from the glass at his side and looking like anything but a man with questions on his mind . . . but appearances, as Maitland knew to his cost, could be deceptive. Sir Nicholas was tall and fair; so fair that any grey there might be in his hair wasn't at all obvious. His air of authority was quite unconscious, nor had he ever been aware of the fact that most of his employees exploited him unmercifully. He was more heavily built than his nephew and his features were a good deal more regular, but in spite of this an observer could occasionally be startled by a faint, elusive likeness between them that was chiefly a matter of expression.

Vera, seated near her husband, turned her head to smile at Antony as he crossed the room. She was a tall woman with a mass of greying hair that was only too liable to escape from the confining pins at the most inopportune moment, and a predilection for dressing herself in drab, shapeless garments. Under Jenny's guidance she was, however, acquiring a sense of colour; just as, under Sir Nicholas's tutelage, she was learning a gentlemanly appreciation of wine.

'Gibbs been pointing out you're late?' she said in her gruff way, which would have frightened Antony to death

60

when he first met and worked with her years ago but which now he took as an expression of sympathy. 'Sorry you got burdened with this Ryder thing,' she continued. 'Still, I suppose as it's Geoffrey's case —'

'I thought that we had decided', said Sir Nicholas, picking up his glass and gazing at the contents as though the only thought in his mind was admiration of the pale straw-coloured liquid therein, 'that you wouldn't agree to this request to sit in on the questioning of the Russian defector.'

'I didn't agree, Uncle Nick.' Antony accepted his sherry and decided that perhaps this evening he would take the chair opposite his uncle's. 'Not in the — the spirit in which the request was made, anyway.'

'I'm glad you added that, I was afraid you were misguided enough to think that in this way you wouldn't be exercising exactly same function.'

'If I ever thought that, I was disillusioned when I told Carr that Geoffrey had persuaded me,' said Antony. Sir Nicholas's tone was too gentle to bode any good, but he couldn't help grinning at the recollection.

'What did he say?' Vera asked curiously.

'Well, old boy, you can weigh him up for us, can't you?' With his unconscious gift for mimicry Maitland reproduced the other man's tone exactly.

'And will you?'

'I didn't say yes and I didn't say no. I expect I will, Uncle Nick,' Antony told him. 'But whether I shall pass on my conclusions —'

'Is that why you took the case?'

'As a matter of fact, no.' He paused, sipping his sherry, and trying to weigh up his own reasons, which were far from clear to him. 'I did it against my better judgement,' he said at last slowly, 'and I think it was mainly because Geoffrey's attitude towards his client was ambivalent and made me feel uneasy. But now I'm glad I agreed.'

'I know very little about the case, of course,' said Sir

Nicholas, 'except the fact of this Dr Gollnow's defection and that he had some information of a highly technical nature about which it was important to know the truth.'

'You know perfectly well what the information is about, Uncle Nick. The Russians are said to be developing charged particle weapons, which I gather is not a good thing, for us at any rate, and I told you all about it when the request for help was first made to me. If it's just a carrot to get Dr Gollnow accepted, so that he can operate as a double agent —'

'I know nothing of such things,' said Sir Nicholas rather loftily. 'However I'll take your word for its importance. You're trying to tell us, Antony, that Geoffrey believes in his client —'

'Not exactly,' said Maitland, much as Horton had done before him.

'Come now, it must be one thing or the other.'

'Not exactly,' Antony repeated, more confidently. 'But he was very much inclined to believe Mrs Ryder when she says her husband couldn't have done such a thing.'

'Faugh!' said Sir Nicholas, to his nephew and niece's intense admiration. 'I've heard you complain about the use of that phrase often enough, Antony.'

'So I have, but —'

'Not like Geoffrey,' said Vera, completing the sentence succinctly for him.

'No, that's why I took some notice.'

'And now you're glad,' said Jenny. 'Does that mean you believe in your new client too?'

'There again I can't give an absolute answer. I just think there are one or two indications . . . and there's also the matter of character.'

'Which I hope you know well enough by this time can be completely misleading.' Sir Nicholas's tone was definitely cold now.

'Yes, but —'

'What he means, Nicholas,' Vera put in, 'is that if there's the faintest chance this man is innocent he ought to do what he can to help him.'

'You know him very well, my dear.' (Perhaps the only thing that annoyed Antony slightly about his uncle's marriage was his and Vera's habit of talking about him as if he were not present.) 'However, as I say, I know nothing about the case. But it isn't like Halloran to go into court without being pretty sure of getting a conviction.'

'I'd say in this instance he's perfectly happy with what he's got.'

'Exactly what information is your client alleged to have been instrumental in handing over. More of these — these charged particle weapons you mentioned?' Vera wondered.

'No,' said Antony, suddenly vague. 'Something to do with green lights.'

'You cannot get up to cross-examine a witness about green lights,' said Sir Nicholas severely. 'The jury will think you're talking about traffic signals.'

'I've got it all written down and if necessary I'll learn it by heart,' his nephew assured him. 'But I very much doubt whether the matter will be mentioned in any detail. After all, why should it be? Exactly what information was handed over doesn't really make any difference to a breach of the Official Secrets Act and I've already told the court the defence don't dispute that aspect of the case.' He paused again, looking all around him. 'Nothing else is classified,' he added.

'Admit I should like to know more about it,' said Vera.

'And so should we all, my dear,' said Sir Nicholas cordially. 'And as the only secret matter appears to concern the Highways Department I think you may safely speak, Antony, and we may safely listen.'

He was looking grave when his nephew finished his story. 'If that is a true representation of the facts, Antony, I think you're mad, quite mad, to undertake this matter at all.'

63

'I seem to have heard that somewhere before, Uncle Nick.' His tone was weary, and Vera and Jenny exchanged a glance, after which Jenny got up quietly and replenished all four glasses. 'Anyway, I don't know what you're making such a fuss about,' Antony went on. 'You can't be afraid this time of my coming up against Superintendent Briggs, the case has nothing to do with him.'

'That is not exactly the point,' said Sir Nicholas, 'though I admit there is a certain amount of gratification to be found in it.'

'It's usually your objection,' said Maitland, finishing his sherry quickly before Jenny reached his side with the decanter. 'Are you telling me I shouldn't have taken the matter on because it's hopeless?'

'On such short notice you were under no obligation . . . *have* you a defence?' Sir Nicholas demanded.

'We shall be calling his employers, by which I mean the head of his department and the company secretary, who seems to be responsible for the senior staff at Wycherley's. And, of course, the chaps who did his security clearance, which is top secret, and who were responsible for keeping it up-to-date, but honestly I don't see what they can tell us. I don't suppose they dogged his footsteps every time he came to London, and even if they did and somebody noticed Dr Gollnow going into Brinkley Court, there are six floors, and twenty flats on each. That would hardly be evidence one way or the other.'

'You said John Ryder's name appeared against the bell for Number 301.'

'Nobody seems to have noticed that and I don't really see why they should have bothered. In any case that would hardly have been incriminating either. I daresay they knew well enough that he stayed at his sister's flat, but they may have thought he changed the name to his own for convenience when she was away.'

'Nothing else?' That was Vera, obviously with some hope

that he was about to pull a rabbit out of a hat.

'His own statement, Vera, his own explanations which I've given you.'

'Do you think the jury will buy them?' In the matter of colloquialisms Sir Nicholas allowed his wife a good deal more latitude than he did his nephew, and he didn't even wince.

'No, I don't.'

'Unless a miracle happens,' said Nicholas didactically, 'I don't see what you can do except watch the matter drift towards its inevitable conclusion.'

'Don't rub it in, Uncle Nick.'

'In any event, why have you changed your mind?'

'I didn't say I had, I said I was wondering.'

'In your case the result is much the same. You will worry yourself about the fate of this John Ryder, who probably deserves all or more than he will get, and in all likelihood you will make a fool of yourself by trying to defend the indefensible. However, I think we should all be interested to know where this doubt you admit to came from.'

Maitland didn't answer immediately. 'I wish I could lay my finger on any one thing myself,' he said at length, 'but quite honesly I can't. All I can say is, it was something about Dr Gollnow's evidence, his identification of John Ryder.'

'He didn't seem sure about it?'

'No . . . no, not that. It was positive enough. Something about it worried me, and all the time he was giving his evidence, talking about the man who had lent his flat for interviews with Nesbit, and introduced them in the first place, too, he didn't sound to my mind as if he was talking about someone who was present.'

'That sounds very much as if you've been letting your imagination run away with you, Antony.'

'You may be right, Uncle Nick,' said Maitland with unaccustomed meekness. 'And there's Ryder himself, the things he told me.'

'He's had plenty of time to think out his answers to the Crown's case,' Sir Nicholas pointed out. He smiled suddenly, first at his nephew and then at his wife. 'As Vera is about to remind me, there have been occasions when you've been right before on equally flimsy grounds. Let us assume for a moment that that is the case here. What do you think you can do about it?'

'Not a damn thing.'

'If you could break down these two identifications, the bigamous wife's and the Russian defector's, where would you stand then?'

'That'd be a different matter, but I can't see any prospect of doing it. I did get Carruthers to agree that Dr Gollnow might be recalled if I had any further questions for him when I'd heard the other evidence, but I can't honestly see what good it'll do. As for the other Mrs Ryder — it must be confusing the hell out of the jury, because no one seems to know whether to call her that or by her maiden name, which is Paull — I shan't know until I've talked to her, of course, but I imagine she's as tough as an old boot.'

'How do you make that out?'

'Supposing John Ryder is innocent . . . give me a chance, Uncle Nick, you said you were willing to assume that for a moment.'

'Very well.'

'Have you thought what follows?'

'Certain things are obvious: That Dr Gollnow is not sincere in his defection, and that the secret he is bringing with him must on no account be trusted. That there is a second John Ryder, who went through a ceremony of marriage with this Winifred Paull — did you say two and a half years ago? — which ceremony may or may not have been genuine. There is also the possibility, I should think a very strong possibility, that this John Ryder did not exist before that time. Whether that is right or not, Miss Paull is

66

lying now to protect him.'

'There's another thing still to be explained, the passport that was found in Number 301. It was quite definitely my John Ryder's, and he doesn't know when he lost it. If, of course, he did lose it.'

'You're saying, I think, that the man who is now on trial has been deliberately framed for this crime.'

'If he's innocent that's the only explanation. I can't go further than that.'

'So what follows?'

'That someone who knew him well and knew of his periodic visits to London deliberately assumed his identity and when the occasion offered pinched his passport to add a little verisimilitude to the story. And that could only have been one of the three men with whom he worked when he came to London. Other people may well have had the opportunity of taking the passport, but nobody else could have known in sufficient detail the particulars of his job in Wolverhampton and his habits when in London.'

'Yes, that seems quite clear. Can you also come up with an explanation of what Dr Gollnow is trying to do?'

'The most likely thing, as I said, seems to be that he has ambitions to become a double agent, and also that he felt it was time Dennis Nesbit was thrown to the wolves. The reason for that escapes me, unless he was becoming remorseful about what he was doing and showed it. And there was no harm in mentioning John Ryder, because there was a Lord High Substitute ready to hand.'

'These three men you mentioned — what were their names?'

'Braithwaite, Walters and Gibbon.'

'They're being called by the prosecution, I believe you said.'

'Yes, Uncle Nick, I did. You know as well as I do that Halloran never leaves anything to chance.'

'Then you must see what you can do in cross-examination. And the same thing, of course, in the case of Miss Paull.'

'And a fat lot of good that will do,' said Maitland frankly. 'The trouble is, Uncle Nick,' he added, before Sir Nicholas could protest at this misuse of the English language, 'I have to admit that I found myself rather liking Dr Boris Gollnow.'

I

Halloran wasted no time the following morning in renewing his examination of Mr K. There was some reiteration, presumably for fear the jury might have forgotten already what had passed the day before, and then they came to the interview with John Ryder, his denials of any knowledge of Gollnow, or Nesbit, or the girl in the London flat, very much as he had told it to his lawyers the evening before.

Mr K. himself had a certain sense of drama, Maitland concluded; his description of the confrontation with Winifred Paull, and later with Boris Gollnow, left nothing to be desired in this connection. Ryder had maintained he had never noticed his own name on the list of tenants at Brinkley Court, there were clothes, mostly of a casual nature, which would have fitted him in the flat he shared with the second Mrs Ryder, and also toilet articles. Nothing at all in Mr and Mrs Mason's flat, which he claimed to have occupied when he was in town. Exhaustive inquiries had been made among the occupants of the block of flats . . .

At this point Halloran raised a hand to silence the witness. 'My lord, my learned friend has agreed that this witness may inform the court of his findings in this direction, without our having to call the people concerned as witnesses. As your lordship will see, it is a very small matter.'

'Very well, Mr Halloran, as we have Mr Maitland's agreement there is no reason why your witness should not continue.'

'Thank you, my lord.' He turned back to Mr K. 'I'm sorry to have interrupted you, but there are certain niceties —'

'Which your friend, Mr Maitland, would be only too pleased to insist on,' said the witness, with a sudden broad grin that completely changed his appearance and reminded Maitland very vividly of their earlier acquaintance, 'if it were not, as you say, a very small matter. A number of people recognised the prisoner from having seen him in the lift, but nobody could remember which floor he got off, and nobody had ever seen him going into either of the flats . . . Number 301 or Number 417.'

'Thank you. Now before I let you go I must ask you, as I see the question hovering on the tip of my learned friend's tongue, whether John Ryder's fingerprints were found in either place?'

'No, they weren't. Number 417, the Masons' flat, had obviously been cleaned very thoroughly, which Ryder explained was his habit when his sister might come home unexpectedly. The same applied to the other flat . . . Miss Paull had occupied herself after the man she thought to be her husband had left her by what she called ''having a good turnout''.'

'That is all I have to ask the witness, my lord, but I'm sure that Mr Maitland —'

Antony was on his feet already. 'This turnout that Mrs Ryder . . . that Miss Paull had indulged in,' he asked, 'had it also removed all traces that Dr Gollnow and Mr Nesbit had ever been in the apartment?'

'Yes, it certainly had.'

'You will forgive me for labouring such a minor point, but are you by any chance implying that Miss Paull's explanation of the lack of fingerprints is more likely than my client's?'

'A woman with time on her hands is more likely —

70

wouldn't you say? — to occupy herself with domestic matters.'

'An opinion which in these days may be regarded as a trifle out of date. Have you any sisters?'

'My lord!' said Halloran, rising to his feet.

'Yes, Mr Maitland, isn't your question a trifle irrelevant?'

'Not at all, my lord. If the witness indeed had a sister, particularly an elder sister, I think he might be aware that trying to keep in her good graces was not always easy. Members of the same family are inclined to be a trifle outspoken with each other and —'

'That will do, Mr Maitland. You may make that point later, when you address the Court.'

'If your lordship pleases. Perhaps I may be permitted to ask what fingerprints were found in the flat taken in John Ryder's name.'

'Only Miss Paull's.'

'Not even on the toilet articles you mentioned, alleged to have been used by my client?'

'Not even on those.'

'Didn't you find that a little strange? It was natural enough for Mr Ryder to pack up everything and leave his sister's flat tidy, but —'

The judge and the witness spoke together. 'I might have found it odd,' said Mr K., 'if it hadn't been for the corroborating evidence of the passport.'

'Mr Maitland!' said Carruthers.

It was he whom counsel chose to answer. 'My lord?' he asked.

'You're doing it again,' said Carruthers rather plaintively.

'Your lordship will forgive me if I say that I don't follow your meaning.'

'Making comments which should more properly be left until you address the jury.'

71

'I apologise, my lord.' He smiled suddenly. 'Perhaps it will assuage my learned friend's natural indignation if I tell you that I have only one more question for the witness.'

'I think,' said Carruthers seriously, 'that might well be the case.'

'Your lordship is most kind.' He turned back to the witness. 'What opinion did you form of Winifred Paull?'

Halloran, not quite so spry as he used to be, thank heaven, was only half way to his feet when Mr K. replied. 'I have no reason to doubt her story, and no evidence of any wrong-doing on her part.' His tone was a trifle grudging, and as a testimonial it carried no conviction at all.

While the witness stepped down and was replaced by his colleague, Mr Y., Derek Stringer turned to his leader and said in a low voice, 'I don't know how you dared ask that last question. The result might have been disastrous.'

'Ah, but you haven't the privilege of a previous acquaintance with Mr K.,' said Antony grinning. 'He's a suspicious old bird, takes nobody at their face value.'

'Just as well. All the same, it was a risk.'

'Well, there was no harm done,' said Maitland pacifically. And turned his attention to the witness, who by now had been sworn in. This was a man he had never seen before, rather younger than his colleague, and his evidence, though it took some time, was of very little interest being merely of a corroborative nature. Maitland didn't even bother to cross-examine.

In fact the rest of the morning turned out to be a dead loss from the point of view of the defence. There was the arresting officer from the Special Branch. There was the hand-writing expert who had been promised, who had no hesitation in stating categorically that the suicide note had been written by Dennis Nesbit. There was Mr Nesbit's secretary, who was equally definite that her employer had been alone all the afternoon in question, his room could only be reached through hers, and she had had instructions to

72

hold all telephone calls. When she found him at five o'clock the letter that had been introduced into evidence was lying on his blotting-pad almost hidden by his body where he had fallen across the desk. She too was in no doubt about the handwriting.

Again neither Maitland nor Stringer indulged themselves in any cross-examination, except to ask whether at any time she had been conscious that documents had been removed from the office and re-filed wrongly. The answer to that was that she had noticed nothing of the sort, but Mr Nesbit had a very careful nature, and if he had removed anything it would certainly not have been beyond him to find the right place to return it. Which helped neither defence nor prosecution.

Over lunch Maitland and Horton in chorus put Derek Stringer in possession of the facts they had gleaned from the interview with John Ryder. 'Which is all very well,' said Derek stringently when they had finished. 'That was all in the brief.'

'Exactly!' said Geoffrey triumphantly.

'You know better than that, Derek,' Antony protested. 'The way people say things is just as important as what they say.'

'Am I to understand that you have now convinced yourself that the man is innocent?'

'No, but I have my doubts.' He went on to explain, much as he had done at home the previous evening, and was amused to note that as his own realisation of the possibility of their client's innocence had increased, Geoffrey's doubts had faded. 'If either of you could convince me of his guilt I'd be grateful,' he assured them. 'As it is, we'll just have to wait and see.'

'Then the witnesses this afternoon', said Geoffrey, 'will be of some interest to you.'

'Ryder's three colleagues in the London office?'

'Yes, and the wives of two of them.'

'I know that, but I can't think what on earth they can have to say to the point.'

Geoffrey sighed elaborately and opened his mouth to reply. 'No, don't bother,' Antony told him. 'I know it's all written down, but I shall have to listen to it all over again this afternoon so you needn't refresh my memory. I take it Halloran's relying on a strong finish with Winifred Paull's evidence. That should be interesting.'

'Only if you could catch her out in a lie, and if your friend Mr K. couldn't I don't suppose for a moment that you can,' said Geoffrey bluntly. 'And for heaven's sake don't start attacking these people this afternoon, they're only innocent bystanders after all and we don't want to alienate the jury.'

'Or Carruthers,' said Antony. 'Or even Halloran for that matter. But you needn't worry, I shall tread as delicately as Agag, and you must admit that having some doubt in one's mind adds a little spice to the situation.'

Geoffrey only grunted at that, and exchanged a glance with Stringer in which there was much of helpless resignation. They concentrated on less contentious subjects for the rest of the meal, and were back in court in good time.

II

Perhaps because of his seniority, Donald Walters was the first witness to be called that afternoon. He was a tall man, a little stooped, but in spite of this looking much younger than his years. He had what Maitland immediately classified in his own mind as an india-rubber face, so that whatever he said his expression echoed his words and lent them a good deal of effect. It didn't take long to reach the meat of his testimony, after he had described the set-up of the London office, and spoken of John Ryder's presence there one week in every three. 'I believe you were in the habit of lunching with the accused on the occasions when he was in town,' said Halloran, with a sidelong look at his adversary which said clearly enough, 'I know I'm leading the witness, but does it really matter?'

Maitland chose to ignore the look, or perhaps he was already completely absorbed in studying the witness. 'That's quite correct,' Donald Walters replied.

'And that you dined together on occasion?'

'Yes.'

'And would I be right in adding, Mr Walters, that no one else was present on these occasions?'

'That is correct in general, and certainly true of all the occasions we dined together. At lunchtime we went to a little place round the corner, somewhere quite simple, and might occasionally run into someone I knew.'

'Still, you must have had the opportunity of getting to know him fairly well.'

'Yes.' There was a faint hesitation. 'But if I'm to be frank with you, our association outside office hours was one of courtesy. I asked him out one night, a little later he returned the invitation, and we went on from there on a strictly reciprocal basis.'

'You had no desire to further the relationship beyond that?'

'There was so great a disparity in our ages,' said Walters, and for the first time turned his eyes towards the still figure in the dock.

'Yes, I understand that. Perhaps you would tell us, Mr Walters, what happened on these evening occasions when you were together? The evenings you asked him out for instance. Did you dine at your home?'

'No, I'm not much of a hand at cooking and prefer to eat out. But we'd leave the office together, go to my place for a drink, and then go out to the restaurant I usually patronise, which is not far from my flat.'

'And on the occasions when Mr Ryder returned your hospitality?'

'We would still leave the office together. He seemed to have a fairly extensive knowledge of restaurants and would choose one with a comfortable bar where we could sit and talk until we were ready for our meal.'

'Are you telling me that you never went to the same place twice?'

'Not quite that, though he was in the habit of ringing the changes. Myself, I prefer to go somewhere where I'm known.'

'And he didn't follow your example in taking you back to his sister's flat for a drink?'

'No, I was never there.'

'Didn't that strike you as a little odd?'

Again the witness hesitated. 'To be frank with you, it did. But of course I can understand why quite well now.'

'Then perhaps you will enlighten us, Mr Walters.'

'Why, this bigamous marriage.' (The newspapers had been busy, Maitland reflected, during the period when John Ryder had been assisting the police — or rather the S.I.S. — with their inquiries.) 'I knew his circumstances perfectly well, that he had a wife in Wolverhampton, and though I think I may say I know how to be discreet, he wouldn't want me to get wind of this other woman.'

At this point Halloran caught Maitland's eye, turned and made a vaguely apologetic bow in the direction of Mr Justice Carruthers and said smoothly, 'But that is to get into the realms of conjecture, is it not, Mr Walters?' Just as though he himself had not invited the comment. 'In the course of your conversations with him,' counsel went on, 'was anything said to lead you to suppose that he was maintaining two establishments?'

'We didn't in general discuss personal matters,' said the witness rather pedantically. 'I remember that he was quite ready to return home early after our evenings together, but as I said, we had really very little in common. But one evening he seemed to forget himself and made some joking reference to getting home to the little woman.'

'You didn't ask him what he meant by that?'

'It would hardly have been tactful. If he was amusing himself it was none of my business.'

'Thank you. Now, Mr Walters, I believe there's one other matter on which you can help us. There was an occasion about two months ago . . . can you be more specific about the date?'

Mr Justice Carruthers leaned forward. 'Hardly, Mr Halloran, unless the witness is told something more about the occasion to which you refer.'

'If your lordship pleases. An occasion, Mr Walters, which may have a bearing on this unhappy business. I'm afraid, my lord,' he added in a sort of aside, 'that if I specify the matter more clearly my learned friend, Mr Maitland, will object.'

'Yes, no doubt he would. Can you help us Mr Walters?' Carruthers asked.

'I can, my lord, but I must make it clear that this is a question I would not wish to answer under oath.'

'Why not?'

'Because it is a question of the identification of a man I saw once in a newspaper photograph, which I'm sure you will agree —'

'Very well, we understand that, and I shall instruct the jury to take cognisance of the fact. Now perhaps you will answer Mr Halloran's question. Can you put a precise date on the event which concerns this man?'

'I'm afraid not, my lord. There was nothing to impress it particularly on my mind. All I can say is that it was an occasion when John Ryder had been entertaining me, and we had dined at Ricardo's, not too far from Brinkley Court. On the way out he paused to greet a man who was entering and I must say he didn't look very pleased to see him. They spoke together for a moment, and I went on ahead. I'm afraid that's all I can tell you.'

77

'But the identification, Mr Walters,' Halloran prompted him. 'We understand your qualms about this, but it may be an important point.'

'It was a man very like Dr Boris Gollnow, whose photograph I saw in the paper when the news of his defection first came out, and before what I presume to have been a news blackout was put on the affair.'

'Thank you very much, Mr Walters.' Halloran's tone was, reasonably enough, sincere. 'I shan't detain you any longer, but I'm quite sure my friend has some questions for you.'

'Not too many.' Maitland came leisurely to his feet. 'You admit, Mr Walters, that this identification of John Ryder's acquaintance as Boris Gollnow is a doubtful one?'

'I'd hoped I had made that clear. Though doubtful isn't quite the right word, because to be frank with you I'm quite sure in my own mind —'

'But not sure enough to swear to the fact,' Maitland interrupted swiftly. 'However, let us go back a little. You seem surprised that a man not permanently resident in London could have a fair knowledge of the restaurants here. Now to my mind that makes good sense. It's the local people who never see the sights, or find the best places to eat, they've no need to. A stranger might get all the information he needed from one of the reference books . . . don't you think?'

'Yes, I suppose so.'

'Did my client never speak to you about his wife?'

'I would make a routine inquiry each week when he arrived, politeness merely. He always answered me that she was well, though I learned recently from — from Mr Gibbon I think — that Caroline Ryder is pregnant.'

'This reference to "the little women". Rather an unlikely phrase, wouldn't you agree?'

'I can only repeat what he said.'

'But you took it quite definitely to refer to someone here in

London, and not to the wife whom you knew about in Wolverhampton?'

'He spoke of getting home.'

'Well, if it was a Thursday night, for instance, he might have been thinking of his reunion with Mrs Ryder — the real Mrs Ryder — the following day?'

'I never dined with him on a Thursday.'

'You sound very sure about that.'

'For some reason it was always towards the beginning of the week.'

'So it couldn't have been Mrs Caroline Ryder he was referring to?'

'If he had been there would have been no need to look embarrassed when he realised what he'd said.'

'Oh, he looked embarrassed, did he? You didn't tell us that.'

'It's true, however. Of course, I never dreamed he'd actually committed bigamy.'

'You thought he was keeping a popsy, and that it was none of your business?' said counsel, forgetting himself for a moment.

'A popsy, Mr Maitland?' said Mr Justice Carruthers, putting down his pen.

'That he was conducting an adulterous relationship,' said Antony, quickly thinking of the stuffiest phrase he could. He turned back to the witness. 'What I can't understand, Mr Walters, is why his not taking you home for a drink before dinner was such a great matter. He had his sister's flat at his disposal, as well — if the prosecution are to be believed — as the one he maintained at Number 301, Brinkley Court.'

'I think the fact that he wasn't living there would have been obvious.'

'And your evenings together generally broke up rather early?'

'They did.'

'Might that not have simply been because he was bored?'

'I hope not,' said Walters rather stiffly. 'Even apart from personal matters, which we avoided, we had plenty to discuss.'

'World affairs? Politics? I suppose, too, that you had a common interest in the company you worked for.'

'All those things and company matters in general, though not detailed matters of technology.'

'Why not?'

'That wasn't his function.'

Maitland smiled at him. 'I think I know already the answer I shall get to this question, Mr Walters, if it were anything but "no" my learned friend would certainly have put it to you already. However, just to make everything quite clear between us, did you ever discuss with him the project on which you were working?'

'No, I didn't. As I said our responsibilities were entirely different. Perhaps I should explain that what my colleagues and I are doing is thinking about possible future projects, deciding on their viability, and then, if the time seems propitious, passing the matter for further study to the laboratory at Head Office.'

'Thank you for explaining that so clearly. The point I'm getting at, however, is that there was no reason why you should not have discussed these matters with John Ryder.'

'Not that I knew of.'

'He was a colleague, with credentials you had no reason for doubting. You never had any suspicion that he might be in touch with . . . I mustn't say the enemy, but with some foreign power?'

'No suspicion in the world. If I had I should hardly have allowed the matter to rest there, but been in touch with security immediately.'

'Yes, I see. Had you had occasion to meet Dennis Nesbit of the Admiralty Underwater Weapons Establishment?'

'As it happens, no.'

'And I gather from your reluctance to make a positive

80

identification that you have no acquaintanceship with Dr Boris Gollnow either?'

'Certainly not.'

'Thank you, Mr Walters. Unless my friend wishes to re-examine —'

Bruck Halloran however declined the invitation. Donald Walters was directed to his place in the body of the Court, where the previous witnesses, with the exception of Dr Gollnow, were sitting. He was replaced in the witness-box a few moments later by a tall, earnest-looking man with bony wrists protruding from the sleeves of a jacket that was a little too small for him, and a pair of steel-rimmed spectacles. His name, it transpired, was Ernest Braithwaite, the second of the trio with whom John Ryder had shared the office in London.

As the direct examination proceeded it became obvious to Maitland that Halloran had no real interest in this group of witnesses. Someone was being just a little too careful, the identifications from Boris Gollnow and Winifred Paull should have been quite sufficient; still, here they were and the prosecution must do what it could with them. Braithwaite confirmed that though he and his wife, Jane, always asked John Ryder home to dinner, when he returned the compliment he took them to a restaurant. Sometimes the Gibbons accompanied them, sometimes there were just the three of them. Yes, he had noticed that they were never asked to Brinkley Court, but Mrs Mason sounded a bit of a Tartar, he didn't wonder John wanted to keep the place looking nice. He smiled then openly, first at the prisoner and then a little apologetically at the judge. 'Jane would say we'd have left everything as we found it,' he confided, 'but John was always a great one for wanting to do things for himself.'

'What did you talk about at these meetings of yours, Mr Braithwaite?'

'Anything, everything. Good heavens, if he could —' He

81

broke off, apparently seeing Donald Walters for the first time. 'I just meant he's quite capable of sustaining a conversation at any level,' he added rather stiffly.

'Did you speak to him of the work you were doing?'

'No, but that wasn't because I didn't trust him. I didn't think he'd be very interested.'

'Even though he had spoken freely to you of his opinions?'

'If you mean that he thought technical and scientific information should be exchanged more freely between the different countries, there are a lot of people who think that, but it doesn't mean they go about disregarding the Official Secrets Act.'

'All the same he was an advocate of freedom of information?'

'Yes, I suppose so. A lot of people think it would make things better, not worse.'

'Do you believe that, Mr Braithwaite.'

'Well, no, but —'

'And yet John Ryder mentioned his own opinion to you on a number of occasions?'

'It didn't mean —'

'Please answer the question, Mr Braithwaite.'

'He did talk about it sometimes, but it didn't mean he was disloyal. I sometimes wondered whether it wasn't just that he enjoyed a good argument.'

'Thank you, that is all.'

Maitland was on his feet, not quite capable of suppressing altogether a certain reprehensible satisfaction at Halloran's discomfiture. 'I don't know how much you know about the evidence in this case, Mr Braithwaite —'

'Damn all,' said the witness frankly.

'— but I gather that on the information you have you don't think it's likely my client is guilty of what the prosecution allege?'

'No, I don't. And Jane doesn't either.'

'Mrs Braithwaite will tell us that herself, I hope, in a few moments. Did Mr Ryder talk about his wife sometimes?'

'Yes, quite often.'

'And you never suspected that he had a woman friend in London?'

'Absolutely not. But if he had, you know, it would explain why he didn't take any of us to Brinkley Court. He might have confided in William or me about it, but he wouldn't want Jane or Edith to know.'

'You've heard of Dr Boris Gollnow. Did you never meet him?'

'No, never.'

'Or Dennis Nesbit, The A.U.W.E. chap who committed suicide?'

'No, I never met him either.'

'Thank you very much, Mr Braithwaite, that is all.'

He hadn't expected Halloran to re-examine and he'd been quite right about that. Jane Braithwaite was taking the oath almost before her husband was settled in his new place, a girl who looked no more than twenty, and whom Antony was later to describe to Jenny as an authentic cherub. Though how much this view of her was coloured by her performance in the witness-box . . .

From the moment the questions began it was clear she was on the defensive and she sounded unwilling as she admitted that what they had been told about John Ryder's habit of entertaining away from home was quite correct. She went on to admit that she didn't always listen very closely, because some of the conversations he had with her husband were man's talk, but he also talked a lot about his wife, Carol, and always with great affection.

'Would you say, Mrs Braithwaite, that he liked women?'

'If I knew exactly what you meant by that I might answer it,' she told him, chin in the air.

'I think, madam,' — Mr Justice Carruthers was inclined to be indulgent — 'that Mr Halloran's question refers to something more than casual friendship. He's asking you whether you felt that Mr Ryder was the sort of man to need a woman in his life.'

('In his bed,' said Maitland to Stringer, for his ears alone.)

'He had Carol.'

'But Mrs Caroline Ryder's company was not always available to him.' Halloran took up the questioning again. 'Would you not agree, Mrs Braithwaite, that his very fondness for her might indicate his need for female companionship in the sense that his lordship has so kindly explained to you?'

'I suppose it might,' she admitted grudgingly. 'I don't happen to believe it, but in any case it doesn't matter, he isn't being tried for bigamy.'

Maitland, who at this point, could quite cheerfully have hugged the witness, declined in this case to cross-examine.

William Gibbon was another tall man, broad-shouldered, dark-haired, who might also have justified the word handsome in his description. As Halloran got through the routine questions Maitland took time to hope that Derek Stringer was taking some care with the note, the witnesses were succeeding one another so rapidly he was almost losing track of which was which. Not that he need have worried, as he should have known, there was never a man who paid more attention to detail than Stringer, which perhaps was what made him such a good foil for his more mercurial leader.

William Gibbon agreed that he and his wife had never been to Brinkley Court and he for one had thought it very odd that John hadn't asked them there. Not for a meal perhaps, that was quite understandable with a temporary bachelor, but they could have gone in for a drink first or even afterwards for a liqueur. But that was John all over, he seemed to like spending money freely, though he was always complaining of being hard up. He'd find a difference when the baby came, and from what he said Carol wouldn't be content with just one. But of course if he was getting money apart from his salary that would make a difference.

One or two nasty implications there, something had better be done about them. 'You wouldn't blame a man for being generous,' said Maitland when his turn came, without preamble.

'No, of course not.'

'I would suggest to you then that there is very little basis for this criticism of my client.'

'I wasn't exactly —'

'A man may choose his priorities. If one of them is to do his best for his friends when he entertains them, is there anything wrong with that?'

'It all depends where the money comes from,' said Gibbon unwillingly.

On the wrong track. Try again. 'You have known my client for some time. Have you ever had reason to distrust him?'

'In the matter of ordinary, everyday honesty —'

'I beg your pardon, Mr Gibbon, that was not exactly what I meant. I meant in his loyalty to his country.'

'Well, no, of course not. He had a security clearance like the rest of us, why should I think there was anything wrong with it?'

'Let us leave aside for the moment the question of his guilt or innocence. You have not all the facts at your disposal to make a decision. But do you think he is the kind of man to do what is alleged of him?'

'I've never thought about it at all. But they don't make mistakes in matters like this, do they?'

'Will you forgive me, Mr Gibbon, if I say that that is an incredibly naïve remark?' The witness looked daggers at him but made no reply. 'The only thing I should like to ask you is whether you ever suspected that he had a woman friend in London?'

'No, though he wasn't indifferent to the ladies. A bit too attentive sometimes, if you know what I mean. But of course he wouldn't try anything on with Jane or Edith, they were the only two I ever saw him with.'

'So, as far as you know, everything was quite regular in his marital relationship with Mrs Caroline Ryder?'

'So far as I know, yes.'

'Do you know, Mr Gibbon, or have you any reason to suppose, that my client was acquainted with Dr Boris Gollnow, or Mr Dennis Nesbit of the A.U.W.E.?'

'I don't suppose I knew all his acquaintances.'

'Perhaps not.' Counsel's tone sharpened. 'But these two people —'

'I'd never heard of either of them until all this started, so naturally I can't say whether John knew them or not.'

'Damn these people,' said Maitland as he sat down again. 'I wouldn't call that an example of great cross-examination, would you?'

'Cheer up,' Stringer advised him, his tone as low as his leader's. 'Mrs Braithwaite did quite well for us, and perhaps Mrs Gibbon will do the same.'

But as soon as he saw her Antony knew that wasn't going to be the case. He wrote ''A hard-faced bitch'' on a scrap of paper, and shoved it across to Derek, who only snorted, 'I can see that for myself,' and crumpled the note up safely. Like her husband, Mrs Gibbon thought it was very odd they'd never been asked to Brinkley Court, she and William had often discussed the matter. And she didn't think John would actually have gone so far as to marry a second time, but she knew he was seeing a girl in London sometimes because she'd seen them together. It was one night when William and she were dining at Ricardo's, where John had taken them sometimes, and John was there with a blonde.

'You didn't point them out to your husband, Mrs Gibbon?'

'No, I didn't like the look of the girl so I didn't want

86

William to see them, it might have ended up with our all sitting together. And I don't think they noticed us.'

'Have you seen this woman again, Mrs Gibbon?'

'Yes, I saw her coming out of Brinkley Court. I was in a car across the street with two plain-clothes men . . . well they're not proper policemen, are they? But still, you know what I mean.'

'And you made a positive identification?'

'Oh yes, I was quite sure it was the same woman.'

This time Maitland could hardly wait for his turn. 'This identification,' he said a little abruptly as the witness turned to face him. 'Tell us exactly what led up to it.'

'They — the men I spoke about — came to see William, and after they'd talked to him they asked me some questions about John.'

'Just one moment, Mrs Gibbon, was this after my client had been arrested?'

'Yes, I knew about that.'

'And had read a report, perhaps, of the Magistrate's Court hearing?'

'Well, naturally I was interested because it was someone we knew,' she replied defensively.

'May I take it, madam, that that is an affirmative answer to my question?'

'Of course I'd read it.'

'So the two men who were investigating the matter talked to you. And then?'

'I told them about this woman.'

'Why did you think that might be relevant?'

'They asked me.'

'What exactly did they say?'

'Oh, well, just if I'd ever seen John with anybody not connected to the office.'

'But you were aware then that the question of his having two wives had arisen?'

'Yes, that came out right at the beginning. Jane said she

87

was sure it was a mistake, but I just thought it must be this woman.'

'Whom your companions told you was another Mrs Ryder?'

'Not until later. After I'd said she was the one I'd seen before.'

'Did you know, had you any means of knowing, that she was the person they were interested in?'

'No, how should I?'

It was Maitland's turn to feel dejected. There'd been no pictures of Winifred Paull in the newspapers, of that he was sure.

'When you first saw them together —?' he began, not a complete change of subject, that might have made his discomfiture too obvious, and she answered without waiting for him to complete the query.

'I thought if he wanted some fun when he was alone he'd a right to it.'

'You'd never any cause to distrust him?'

'So far as women were concerned —'

'That wasn't what I meant exactly, madam. As far as his loyalty to his country was concerned.'

'Well no, but that's hardly something I'd know about, is it?'

'Did you enjoy the restaurants my client took you to?'

'Of course I did. That's why William and I went back to Ricardo's when we thought we'd have a night out together.'

'No complaints about the extravagance of your entertainment?'

'Well no, though I did wonder sometimes . . . but that's all explained now, isn't it?'

'I wonder,' said Maitland, and found the judge's eyes on him as he sat down again.

Maitland was conscious of a quickening of excitement as the next witness was called. Not that the testimony he had been hearing since lunch hadn't interested him. It had . . . very much indeed, but he wanted time to sort out his impressions. Meanwhile, here was a girl who had either been deeply wronged or was a consummate liar, and there was always a chance, a very faint chance . . .

His first thought was that John Ryder had been inaccurate in describing her as brassy, an adjective which he took to apply not only to the colour of her hair but also to her manner. She was certainly fair, though very little of her hair was showing under the tight-fitting hat she wore, which — like her coat — was a sober shade of blue. As to her style, the description didn't fit that either. At first she kept her eyes modestly cast down, and spoke in so low a tone that Halloran, his own booming voice muted for the moment, had to ask her to speak up.

'I know this must be very difficult for you, madam,' he said, 'but we must be able to hear what you have to say.'

At that she looked up at him, and from there on her answers came clearly enough. Yes, her name was Winifred Paull, and she still lived at Number 301, Brinkley Court. And yes, she recognised the prisoner as the man with whom she had gone through a civil ceremony of marriage on the fifth of October, 1971, though she showed some signs of distress as she added, 'I really thought we were married until it was proved to me recently that at that time he had a wife already. And it's very difficult to believe . . . I loved him, you see.'

While the witness was recovering herself, and sipping the glass of water handed to her by the usher, Halloran took the opportunity of introducing into evidence the marriage certificate, and the lease of the flat signed Winifred Ryder. 'Please believe me, madam,' he said then, turning again to the witness, 'we have no desire to make this any more painful to you than we must. But it is very necessary that you tell the court of your relationship with John Ryder from the beginning.'

'We met in July, July of the year we were married. I was living in Earls Court, a place that called itself a Woman's Club, but my room wasn't very comfortable and I generally went out in the evening. I met John in a cinema queue, we got talking and then we sat together. And after that we saw each other each time he was in town.'

'How soon was marriage discussed between you?'

'On his very next visit. I thought, of course, that he was as much in love as I was,' she added with a sob. 'There was the question of the time required to get the licence, things like that. I'm not a bit surprised the people at the Registry Office couldn't recognise either of us later, they must see thousands of people in the course of a year, but of course there's the certificate so I suppose it doesn't really matter. Or wouldn't have done if . . . well, you're not interested in that. And we had to find somewhere to live.'

'Who suggested Brinkley Court?'

'John did. He said his sister and her husband had a flat there, only they were aboard at present, but he had visited them and it was convenient and comfortable and not too expensive.'

'One moment, Miss Paull. Did he say he was staying at his sister's?'

'No, though he used that address to establish residence. He was staying at an hotel quite near to his office.'

'Can you confirm that statement? Did you ever visit him there?'

'No, there was no occasion for that. So when John went back to Wolverhampton I went round to Brinkley Court, and there happened to be a flat to rent on the second floor and so I took it. It was just what we wanted, two bedrooms. We only needed one, of course, but John had said he must have a study, somewhere to keep his things.'

'You took the flat in you own name?'

'In my married name. I explained to them how soon the wedding would be coming off, and that we wouldn't be moving in until after that, so they agreed I could sign the lease then.'

'John Ryder had nothing directly to do with the arrangement?'

'No, except that he paid the rent.'

'We'll come to that in a moment, Miss Paull. Didn't that strike you as rather odd?'

'No, not really. We'd talked over the question of where we should live, I mean whether I should move to Wolverhampton, or whether we'd stay in London, and as I much preferred the latter and he said he was due for a move at any time we thought that was the best thing to do. Only, of course, he was officially stationed in Wolverhampton, and his bank accounts were there, so he just gave me the money in cash and let me make all the arrangements.'

'Including opening a bank account near your new address?'

'Yes, it seemed simpler that way.'

'And you were satisfied with the explanation he gave you for his frequent absences?'

'Yes, I was. Do you think it was very silly of me? I never thought . . . I loved him so much . . . I never thought he'd be telling me lies.' She paused there and dabbed her eyes again.

'I'm sure we all agree that your attitude was very natural.' Maitland was amused to note that Halloran was almost cooing at his witness now, and Bottom's absurd phrase ran through his mind: *I will roar you as gently as any sucking dove.* 'Let us go on to your marriage then,' counsel's carefully muted voice went on. 'You saw this man whom you believed to be your husband one week in three?'

'Yes, he'd arrive on Sunday evening, and go back most weeks on the last train on Friday.'

'Didn't that strike you as strange, Miss Paull? Surely he could have stayed over the weekend, at least until Sunday.'

'No, there were things, a report he had to write when he

91

got back, and if he left it until Monday it would have been too late. I think he always worked Saturday morning and quite late into the afternoon. At least that's what he told me,' she added in a rather helpless tone.

'Thank you, that's all very clear. Now, during these visits of his, did you have many friends visiting you, did you dine out very often?'

'As for dining out, no we didn't. I suppose', she added rather desolately, 'I was enjoying playing house. I'd see my own friends during the weeks John was away, that was one way of trying to keep from being too lonely, and he hadn't many friends in London yet. Just two men who were regular visitors, and always came on the same evening.'

'The same day of the week do you mean?'

'No, the same evening as each other. It was business of some kind, I think. They'd come after dinner and always spend an hour or so in John's study.'

'Were you ever present on any of these occasions?'

'Not in the study. When they'd finished talking their business they'd come out and we'd all have a drink together. They were really very nice and I quite enjoyed the company, but of course, seeing so little of John I was glad that we didn't have someone every night.'

'Were you told the names of these mysterious gentlemen?'

'Yes, of course. *I* never thought there was anything mysterious about them. One was Mr Nesbit — John always called him Dennis — the other a foreign gentleman, Dr Gollnow. I think his first name was Boris.'

And that was really all, except that Halloran saw to it that his witness had several more opportunities of displaying emotion, so that Maitland was at last moved to protest. 'My lord,' he said, 'I'm beginning to think that my learned friend has mistaken the nature of the case he is prosecuting.' He encountered a look from Halloran, half furious, half astonished, and went on blandly, 'Whether or not there was a bigamous marriage has nothing to do with my client's guilt or innocence of the crime of which he is accused.'

Mr Justice Carruthers thought about that for a moment. 'You're quite right, Mr Maitland,' he said at last. 'Mr Halloran, have you any further questions pertinent to this matter?'

'I think enough has been said, my lord, though there is one question I should like to repeat if your lordship will permit it.'

'What is it, Mr Halloran?'

'The identification of the prisoner by this lady as the man she believed she married, and who was in the habit of meeting Dennis Nesbit and Dr Boris Gollnow at the home they shared.'

'It is certainly pertinent. If you feel Miss Paull should repeat her evidence on that point —'

'I'm obliged to your lordship. Miss Paull, in view of the importance of the question I hope you will not mind answering it again. Do you see the man you believed you had married, with whom you lived as his wife for some time, and who introduced Mr Dennis Nesbit and Dr Boris Gollnow to you as his friends, in this court?'

'Of course I do. That's John' — she was pointing at the prisoner — 'and I wish now', she added, 'that I'd denied everything from the beginning. I didn't want to hurt him, but when those two men came to see me I'd no idea what it was all about.'

'Thank you, madam, you've been very helpful and the court is grateful,' said Halloran. 'I have no further questions for the witness, my lord, but perhaps Mr Maitland —'

Maitland was already on his feet, anticipating his cue. 'Most certainly I have questions,' he said, though truth to tell, now it was growing so late, he would have been glad enough to postpone his cross-examination until the morrow. But so far Carruthers had showed no sign of wishing to adjourn, and that probably meant he'd get half-way through, have to break off, and start again in the morning. 'Since my learned friend', he said, 'has chosen to stress the details of your marriage to a man called John Ryder, I should like to point out to you, madam, that your word is the only evidence we have that my client is the man concerned.'

Halloran was half-way to his feet when the witness spoke rather quickly. 'There's the certificate,' she said, 'and of course we both signed the register.'

'If you have indeed lived with my client for so long, even in the spasmodic way you describe, you are surely aware that the signature in the register is a quite unidentifiable scrawl, not at all like the usual rather clear way he signs his name.'

'If that's a question, why should I know?' Her voice had become a little shrill. 'I've seen his handwriting of course, but lots of people have a very queer signature.'

'Did he never write to you?'

'No. When he was in Wolverhampton he telephoned every night. It was usually about half-past five or six, so I think now that he must have been on his way home to that other woman.'

'Where did you think he was living?'

'In digs, not far from his office.'

'Surely he gave you an address and telephone number.'

'I told you he always called me.' He thought he was getting her measure now; accustomed to her own way, and liable to turn sulky if crossed. 'I could always phone him at work in case of emergency.'

'Did you ever do so?'

'No.' The modest, eyes-cast-down look was back again. 'I didn't want to disturb him.'

'Just an old-fashioned girl, in fact.' He felt rather than saw Halloran's movement and added quickly, though with barely disguised cynicism, 'I'm sure we should all admire

94

such consideration.'

'I just didn't want to be a nuisance,' she flashed at him.

'I see. You say there is no one else who can identify my client as the John Ryder who was living with you at Number 301, Brinkley Court?'

'Nobody now except Dr Gollnow. Of course, Mr Nesbit could have done.'

'You didn't introduce him to any of your friends?'

'It's as I said, I used to meet them when he was away.'

'Not even during the period of your courtship?'

'No, we had so little time.'

'Seriously, madam, I must agree with you there. Perhaps if we tried we could work out the exact date you met by going back three weeks at a time from the date of the alleged marriage.'

'My lord,' said Halloran, 'if my friend wishes again to examine the documents —'

'Thank you, my lord, it will not be necessary. Mr Horton was very properly supplied with copies. In any event the exact date is immaterial. Will you agree, madam, that meeting only at three week intervals you had very little time to get to know one another before the actual date of the wedding?'

'Some people aren't so cold-blooded . . . like a snake,' she added, with a venomous look at counsel, who appeared to sustain it with equanimity. 'We fell in love right away and decided to get married. That was all.'

'You were living in Earls Court at that time. How did you support yourself?'

'I had a job like everyone else.'

'Could you give us a few more details of this occupation, madam?'

'I worked in a flower shop; it's a nice sort of job.'

'And the name of the shop?'

'The Flower Basket. It was quite near the club where I lived. Closed now, I heard the lady had died.'

'And the arrangement you made with your husband about money didn't strike you in any way as strange?'

'Not then.'

'You were completely dependent on the man you were living with?'

'I thought —'

'Were you, Mrs Ryder?'

'Why shouldn't I depend on my own husband?'

'I see,' said Maitland again, ignoring the question. 'How are you living now?'

'Why, I —' Her eyes went towards Halloran in frantic appeal, as though he were the only one in the court that she could trust.

Maitland pressed his advantage. 'The man you say was supporting you is under arrest. How are you living since the payments stopped coming in?'

'I have savings of my own in the account with the other money. I think I was perfectly entitled to use any of it even if he got what he gave me by . . . by doing wrong. I've been through enough, God knows. It hasn't been very nice, let me tell you, telephone calls and such. And one woman even came to the flat on some flimsy excuse.'

'And when the money runs out?'

'I suppose I shall look for another shop to work in. I'd like it to be flowers again, but jobs aren't always so easy to find.'

'Then let us turn to the two friends who did visit the flat. Did the man you knew as John Ryder give you any details of their occupation?'

'My lord!' said Halloran, popping up with unwonted vigour.

'No, Mr Halloran, I think not,' said Carruthers judiciously. 'Perhaps, Miss Paull, you would be kind enough to answer the question.'

'Yes, my lord.' Rather than reassure her the interruption seemed to have made her more nervous. 'I didn't know any details of what they did, except I thought they had some

96

business association with John. Otherwise why shut me out? And why did they both always carry briefcases?'

'We'll leave it at that then.' That was Maitland, taking up the questioning again. 'We have heard evidence that during the weeks he spent in London my client generally dined once with one or other of his colleagues. Did *your* John Ryder leave you alone one evening of each week you spent together?'

'Of course he was out at least once each visit. Business, he said.'

'An extraordinarily trusting disposition,' murmured Maitland, as though to himself. 'Now, Mrs Ryder, you say that except on these occasions you generally ate at home —'

'You mustn't call me that. You know quite well I wasn't really married to him.'

'My lord,' said Halloran, 'this line of questioning is surely causing unnecessary distress to the witness. Would it be too much to ask that my learned friend should address her by her correct name?'

'Yes, Mr Maitland, why don't you call the lady Miss Paull? You have not done so once during the course of your cross-examination as far as I recall.'

'No, my lord, and with reason. To do so would be to admit that the marriage ceremony she went through was bigamous, that the man concerned was in fact my client. It is our case that the man she married, though using the name John Ryder, was not the man you see in the dock.'

There was a moment of stunned silence, and then the witness, who had been given a chair, crumpled sideways and one of the ushers rushed to her assistance.

'I am sure, Mr Maitland,' said Mr Justice Carruthers dryly, 'that your learned friend Mr Halloran will be grateful for enlightenment on this point. However, as the witness seems to be unwell I will adjourn the court until tomorrow morning, when perhaps the rest of your cross-examination can be conducted — shall we say, a little more tactfully?'

97

III

'What in heaven's name did you want to attack the girl like that for?' Geoffrey demanded. He had held his fire until the three of them were safely back in Maitland's room in chambers, but now he seemed to be able to contain himself no longer and spoke with unusual vigour.

'I thought it would be a good idea,' said Antony mildly. The very quietness of his tone should have been enough warning, but Geoffrey for the moment was too angry to notice.

'I thought we were lucky to get old Carruthers because he's always had a soft spot for you,' he said, 'but now you've put his back up. Along with making the jury hate your guts, which is even more important. Why in heaven's name did you do it?' he repeated.

'I've a perfect right to cross-examine any of the prosecution's witnesses,' said Maitland, still mildly.

'Yes, but not if it's going to lose you everyone's sympathy. Look at it for a moment. You know and I know that whether the chap committed bigamy or not is irrelevant, but it's going to be taken into consideration in the jury room, you can count on that. Don't you agree with me, Derek?'

Stringer's eyes were on his leader. 'On the face of it, yes,' he said. 'But Antony still hasn't answered your original question.'

'If you mean why did I try to make things a little hot for Miss Paull or Mrs Ryder or whatever you like to call her,' said Antony, 'I don't like poor little helpless women. Particularly if they're obviously nothing of the kind,' he added.

'She may have been acting up a bit,' Geoffrey admitted.

'Or just have thought that was the right way to behave in

court,' Derek supplemented his statement.

'I don't believe a word of it,' said Maitland flatly.

'Not again!' said Geoffrey, and groaned.

'I don't quite know what you mean by that. You were the one who originally seemed to have some doubts about our client's guilt,' Maitland pointed out; the second part of that statement confirming an understanding which he had denied in the first.

'Yes, but look at the facts as they've been coming out today,' Geoffrey expostulated. 'Miss Paull is in no doubt about the identification any more than Dr Gollnow is. As for the other witnesses this afternoon —'

'I can't think why Halloran called any of them,' said Maitland disagreeably.

'I thought you were looking forward to a chance to weigh them up.'

'Yes I was, but Halloran knew nothing of it and would have been the last person to oblige me if he had. I just don't see what good it did his case.'

'Here a little and there a little,' said Derek Stringer lightly. 'If what they had to say weighed with Geoffrey as it certainly weighed with me, I think you may take it that the jury would be impressed too. After all, the everyday details of people's lives are much more understandable than all this obscure stuff about handing over state secrets and so on.'

'I suppose you're right. Anyway, Geoffrey, we'd better call a truce because there are one or two things I want you to put in hand.'

'You'd better tell me first what you intend to do tomorrow morning.'

'Play it by ear, I suppose.'

'That's no answer.'

'It's all I can give you at the moment. First, I want to talk to John Ryder before the court opens.'

'I can arrange that.'

'Yes, of course you can. Then I want you to get hold of

Cobbold's,' (Cobbold's was the firm of Inquiry Agents that Geoffrey's firm generally used, and whom they found reliable), 'and get them to ask at Ricardo's if our client was ever seen there with a woman. If he was . . . well, they'll know what questions to ask. Then I'd like them to put someone on to tracing Winifred Paull's past before her marriage. Was there ever a flower shop with the improbable name she quoted? Is the owner really dead? Is there anybody else who could remember her at that time? But I don't really need to spell it out for you.'

'No, I see well enough what you're getting at. You've decided the woman was lying.'

'Have a heart, Geoffrey! When we were in court just now everything seemed quite simple. Now . . . you may be right that I've made a mess of the whole affair. Let's leave it at that, shall we, for this evening?'

To this Horton agreed rather grudgingly and left a moment later in Stringer's company. 'That's not what's worrying him,' he said as they went down the rather ill-lit staircase. 'I mean, if Ryder's guilty he deserves all he gets, and though in any event he's entitled to the best defence we can give him I don't suppose Antony would shed any tears over what happens. But his attack on Miss Paull today wasn't a trivial matter, it was tantamount to an accusation of perjury, and by inference perhaps to something even worse. If he was wrong I don't think he'll forgive himself very easily.'

'There's nothing we can do about it in any event,' Stringer assured him. 'Let's all sleep on the question, things may look brighter in the morning. Will you give me a ring first thing and tell me what time they'll have Ryder ready to see us.'

'He's got you curious now,' said Geoffrey, almost accusingly.

'Do you wonder? Good-night, Geoffrey, and don't lose any sleep over the matter. I shan't. But I shouldn't count too much on Antony having a good night,' he added to himself as they parted in the court below.

IV

'I do not believe', said Sir Nicholas, 'that, incautious as you may have been at times, you have ever in the past carried your zeal in your client's interests to such lengths. To induce a loss of consciousness in the witness you were examining —'

'Cross-examining,' Vera corrected him in her gruffest tone.

'You're quite right, of course, my dear,' said Sir Nicholas cordially, 'though I cannot see that it makes the action any less inexcusable.'

After his conference, Antony had lingered a while in chambers and arrived home finally a little later than usual. It didn't need Gibbs's reproachful look or the information that 'Sir Nicholas would like a word with you, Mr Maitland', to turn his steps in the direction of the study door, which stood invitingly open. He'd been only too glad when he got into the room to see Jenny was already installed on the sofa in front of the fire.

'If you don't mind, Uncle Nick,' he said now wearily, 'I had enough of that from Geoffrey. Not to speak of Derek's opinion, though he didn't say so much, that isn't his way. And if you don't mind,' he added noticing that each one of them was already supplied with sherry, 'I'll get myself a drink.'

'Help yourself, my dear boy.' Sir Nicholas waved an inviting hand. 'And then you can tell us —'

'Halloran telephoned, I suppose.' Antony was busy with the decanter and did not look round as he spoke.

'Did you expect anything else? He is rather of the opinion that your sanity has finally forsaken you, and that I should

101

have warning of the fact.'

His nephew was smiling faintly as he came back to join the group by the fire again. 'I'm not going to run amok and wipe out the household,' he said lightly, but none of his hearers was in any doubt that he was at that moment very far from being amused. If nothing else, the stiff way he was holding himself would have told its own story. He was tired, and his shoulder was paining him, and his self-confidence had reached its lowest ebb. 'If that's what's worrying you,' he said, and sat down beside his wife.

'Not precisely,' his uncle told him, but before he could continue Vera had interrupted him.

'Thing is,' she said, 'been a good deal of excitement about this case, what with Mr X. and Mr Y. and all that.'

'Mr K. and Mr Y.,' said Antony precisely and drank some of his sherry.

'Whatever they're calling themselves. That isn't the point. Never done a thing like this before,' said Vera, shaking her head at him.

'I tried to explain that last night.'

'You told us of some uncertainty that had arisen in your mind,' said Sir Nicholas. 'As you felt then, I should have thought the last thing in your mind would have been to attack a witness so forcefully, particularly a witness who, according to Halloran, had established some claim on the jury's sympathy.'

'I daresay it was unwise. I told you, Geoffrey's already spoken his mind on that subject.'

'Unwise? It was sheer insanity,' said Sir Nicholas forcefully.

'Don't you think, Uncle Nick, you'd better let Antony explain,' Jenny put in.

'I've been waiting for him to do so ever since he came home.'

'Yes, but don't you see, something else must have happened to make him realise he was right to be doubtful about this Mr Ryder's guilt. After all, we've heard nothing that went on in court today, except that Mr Halloran admitted that Antony had dealt very well with the witnesses until the last one.'

'Precisely! Until the last one,' said Sir Nicholas. 'Well, Antony? What made you decide finally that your client is innocent?'

'I don't quite know.'

'Come now, that's no sort of an answer.'

'I'm afraid it's the best I can do. All I can tell you —' He broke off there and paused for a moment. 'This morning's witnesses were concerned with corroborating things that had been established already. This afternoon was more interesting, the men from the London office of Ryder's firm.'

'And what they said convinced you —?'

'No, it didn't. Oh lord, Uncle Nick, don't you see I wish it had?'

'In that case —' Sir Nicholas broke off in his turn and glanced at his wife. 'I'm not sure how all this strikes you, Vera, but as for me, I'm more confused than ever.'

'There were things about their evidence, nothing I could put my finger on. Geoffrey, and Derek, too, I think, felt the small points they made were very strongly in support of Halloran's case. I can only tell you that when I got up to talk to that girl —'

'Well?'

'It all seemed quite clear for the moment, what I had to ask her, the whole tone of the cross-examination. Just then I *knew* she was lying, it was only afterwards when we were back in chambers and Geoffrey said his piece that I realised I wasn't sure about anything any more.'

'I see. I expect Geoffrey asked you, too, what you intend to do tomorrow morning.'

'Yes, he did. I told him the first thing was to talk to Ryder again, see what answers he has for the points that arose today. It wasn't a case of their not coming up to proof, you know, but in some cases of going beyond it. So I don't think I can possibly decide — can I? — until I've done that.'

'No, I suppose not. If you want my advice, my dear,' he added with one of the swift changes of mood that would have bewildered anyone who knew him less well than Jenny, 'I'd take your husband upstairs and feed him. He'll feel better for a meal. And afterwards perhaps you'll both join us for a night-cap. I'd like to hear the full story of today's evidence.'

Jenny looked to see if Antony had finished his sherry and then got to her feet. 'We'll come back, Uncle Nick, if you promise not to be horrid,' she said. 'I think Antony was quite right in what he did, after all the wretched girl wouldn't have fainted if she hadn't had something on her conscience.'

Vera and Sir Nicholas exchanged a look as the two younger people left them. Jenny in a militant mood was not altogether strange to them, but Jenny uttering an uncharitable remark about even the blackest of villains was so much out of character as to be completely unknown to them.

V

So, later that evening the tale was told again, and though it sounded meagre even to Antony's ears, paradoxically the re-telling of it went some way towards removing his uncertainties. Before they left the telephone rang and Vera went across to the desk by the window to answer it. 'For you, Antony,' she said, turning and holding out the receiver invitingly. 'I think it's Geoffrey Horton.'

She was right about that. 'When I didn't get you at home I thought I'd chance finding you there,' he said as soon as he heard Maitland's voice. 'Something's happened that I think you ought to know about.'

'What now?' Antony's tone was resigned.

Perhaps some of Geoffrey's earlier annoyance lingered, in any event he made no attempt to wrap up his news. 'Winifred Paull's dead,' he said baldly.

'But she only —'

'Don't worry. She only fainted, you're quite right, you didn't drive her into having a heart attack or anything like that.' That was said more reassuringly, but there was no way of softening the stark facts that followed. 'She was killed at about seven o'clock this evening, and the police have arrested Carol Ryder for her murder.'

THURSDAY, *The Third Day of the Trial*

I

When Maitland arrived the next morning for the interview Geoffrey had arranged, he was relieved to see that Horton and Stringer were already with their client, and that the news of his wife's arrest had already been broken to John Ryder. From the rather quizzical look Geoffrey gave him he gathered that the solicitor had a very good idea that his lateness was intentional, with this very point in mind.

It was interesting to note that Caroline Ryder's predicament had had a far more devastating effect on her husband than his own arrest had seemed to do. He was in the middle of an impassioned tirade, and barely paused to greet his counsel before continuing, 'I don't understand. How could anybody think that Carol —?'

'She was there,' said Geoffrey flatly. And then, 'Look here, let's sit down, all of us, and I'll go over the whole thing again. Mr Maitland and Mr Stringer have had only the barest details from me so far.'

'Very well.' Ryder sat down obediently, but he still looked about as relaxed as a coiled spring. 'I thought yesterday —' he said, and broke off, looking round from one to the other of them helplessly. 'You'll know what to do,' he said, addressing the remark to the three of them indiscriminately.

'Then let us hear what Mr Horton has to say first,' said Antony. 'We have to consider, too, how Miss Paull's death affects your case.'

'That's not important at the moment. Carol is. But I'd be

106

glad to hear it all again because I still don't understand —'

'I'm quite sure it must have been a shock to you.'
Maitland turned to Geoffrey. 'I gather that Mrs Ryder got
in touch with you last night.'

'Yes, she said she didn't know anybody else to turn to in
London.'

'What about the Magistrate's Court hearing?'

'I asked Stanley to take it. That's my partner,' he added
in an aside to their client. 'There was nothing whatever to
be done except reserve her defence; the facts that will be
adduced at this stage aren't under dispute.'

'I see. What time did this happen?' Maitland asked.

'I got a telephone call from her just about eight o'clock,
before eight o'clock I believe. She was . . . distressed,' said
Geoffrey carefully. 'But I was able to gather that Winifred
Paull was dead, and that she wanted me to go to Brinkley
Court immediately. So I did.'

'And you found?'

'The police in possession. I think, to tell you the truth,
they were thoroughly scared of the whole matter, because of
Miss Paull being a witness in a case that was Special
Intelligence business, nothing really to do with them. So
Scotland Yard had been called, and meanwhile Mrs Ryder
hadn't been questioned. I was able to talk to her in the
study . . . the room where the photocopying-machine and
the filing-cabinet were discovered.'

'That was a bit of luck anyway,' said Maitland, and
didn't add, for the sake of John Ryder's feelings, 'from the
sound of things you needed all the luck you could get.'

'What she had to tell me was very simple, but
unfortunately it didn't help matters much. She was in court
yesterday, though I never noticed her. Did you know that,
Mr Ryder?'

'No, I didn't. I never even looked towards the public
gallery.'

'Well, I told you she was concerned for you,' Geoffrey
reminded him. 'And she looked on your cross-examination

of Miss Paull, Antony, in a rather different light from the one in which I saw it, particularly when it ended so dramatically. So she thought perhaps — I'm just repeating what she told me — that if she went to see her right away, while she was still off-balance as it were, she might be able to persuade her to tell the truth.'

'That means she doesn't think I'd been having an affair with that woman,' said John Ryder. 'At any other time that would have been the best news you could bring me.'

'She said, "If I hadn't believed John before, I would have done once I saw her," ' said Geoffrey precisely. ' "She may have deceived all you men with that demure look she put on, but I saw through her in a minute." But to get back to the facts of Mrs Ryder's story. She walked about a bit after leaving the court, getting up her nerve, and then she thought perhaps she'd better get a meal before going to Brinkley Court because the kind of place she could afford might be closed by the time she left again.'

'But there was money in the deposit account . . . for the baby,' said Ryder quickly. 'I hope she hasn't been letting herself go hungry.'

'So she went to a little place not far from her destination,' said Geoffrey, forbearing to point out that the question was no longer material. 'She had some fish and chips and a cup of tea, and she didn't think she could even remember which waitress served her if she saw her again, she was so preoccupied, but of course I'm having inquiries made and there's always a chance the waitress may remember her. But I'm afraid it's hardly likely, even if she did, that she noted the exact time Mrs Ryder left, and as Brinkley Court was so very near I'm afraid an alibi is out of the question, the most we shall be able to do is to suggest that the time might have been rather short for what she is said to have accomplished. In any event she went to the block of flats, read the notice board and pressed the buzzer for 301. There wasn't any reply, but just then some other people were coming in, obviously tenants as they had their own key. She just followed them through the entrance door and into the lift. They were still in it when she got off at the second floor.'

'Could she describe these people?' Maitland asked.

'No, I'm afraid . . . she was very concentrated on what she was doing, not really noticing what went on around her. And to get a little ahead of my story, I learned later that the police inquiries haven't turned them up so far. I expect she slipped in as unobtrusively as she could, and how many times do you remember the face of someone you just saw in the lift?'

'Does that matter?' asked Ryder anxiously.

'It means we can't prove that Winifred Paull didn't press the entry button and let her in herself,' said Geoffrey. 'And that's rather a material point. When Mrs Ryder got to the door of 301, which is at the end of the corridor, she found it standing slightly ajar. She called out —'

'What did she say?'

'Just, "Miss Paull?" She says she called several times and when there was no answer she pushed the door a little. I believe the lay-out in all the flats is identical, there's no hall, you go straight into the living-room. So when she took a step forward and pushed open the door a little further she saw Miss Paull immediately, lying on the rug between the sofa and the television set. That's where, according to her story, she made her mistake.'

John Ryder came to life at that. 'Carol doesn't tell lies,' he said hotly.

'I'm sorry, Mr Ryder. It was not my intention to give that impression, but you told me — didn't you? — before Mr Maitland arrived that you would like him and Mr Stringer to act for your wife.'

'Yes I did, of course I did, but —'

'Then I have to make him understand very clearly what facts can be corroborated, and what stand on your wife's word alone. Do you understand?'

'I suppose I do.'

'Then let me continue. Very naturally, Mrs Ryder's first

thought was that Miss Paull had fainted again, as she had seen her do in court. She went across the room quickly, and it was only then that she saw that her hair was sticky with blood, and when she turned her a little — for she was lying on her face — she saw a deep gash in her right temple. Mrs Ryder has no experience of violent death, she told me, and didn't know whether Miss Paull was actually dead or not.' He paused there and glanced at Maitland, who was frowning, and who shook his head slightly as though to discourage any comment at that point.

'Mrs Ryder's first thought was to telephone for help,' Horton went on, 'but the first thing her eye fell on was a piece of Eskimo carving that had been put down quite neatly on the table near the instrument. I can tell you now that it was the murder weapon; there were blood and hairs on it, and some of the blood transferred itself to Mrs Ryder's hand when she picked it up and turned again to look at Miss Paull. She was horrified of course, but as she tells it the main feeling she had was a mixture of being dazed and being puzzled. And at that exact moment Miss Paull's neighbour from Number 320, whose front door faces hers, walked in. He had heard Mrs Ryder cry out and thought something must be wrong, and you can imagine what the tableau that presented itself looked like to him.'

'Oh, my God,' said John Ryder, and buried his face in his hands.

Geoffrey took a moment to look at him with some evidence of sympathy, but he hadn't finished his story yet. 'I gave Mrs Ryder the only advice I could, to tell her story to the police exactly as she had told it to me. It was some time before the chaps from the Yard arrived — your old friends Sykes and Mayhew, Antony — and evidently the doctor who had done the preliminary examination, and found Miss Paull dead incidentally, was quite convinced that the killing had been done not long before, not earlier than six-thirty at any rate. They canvassed the neighbours before they took any action, but you can guess the answer to that. Everyone was minding his own business, and no one had seen anything.'

John Ryder raised his head. 'But why should anyone think that Carol would have done such a thing?' he asked. 'Whatever the evidence, she'd have to have a motive.'

'I'm afraid,' said Antony, 'there are a number of motives that the prosecution might suggest. Jealousy of the other Mrs Ryder, for instance.'

'But Mr Horton says she didn't believe I was unfaithful to her.'

'That's opinion, nothing more. But let's take the possibilities a little further. She was convinced of your innocence, and furious with Winifred Paull for lying about you. Or perhaps she believed you guilty, but loved you so much she was desperate to see you acquitted. She might have believed that without Winifred Paull's testimony there would be a better chance of that. A— I'm sorry to rub it in, Mr Ryder — but the fact that she's carrying your child might lend weight to any of those suppositions.'

'I hadn't thought of it that way. We were so looking forward . . . and now it looks as if the baby will be born in prison.'

'Then we must see that doesn't happen,' said Maitland briskly.

'You mean you'll help her?'

'To the best of my ability. Provided, of course, that Mr Horton will consent to send me a brief,' he added, smiling a little in an attempt to lighten the atmosphere.

At least John Ryder was thinking again. 'The circumstances will be taken into account, won't they? I mean, her pregnancy, and the terrible strain she's been under with all this. In the ordinary way she's such a gentle person —'

'Wait a bit, Mr Ryder! You're going a good deal too fast for me. I wasn't talking about defending your wife on a plea of diminished responsibility or anything like that. From what Mr Horton tells us her instructions will be to plead Not

Guilty, and we'll proceed on those lines and no others.'

Ryder looked at him for a long moment. 'Thank God,' he said.

'Do you believe she's guilty, Mr Ryder?'

.'Just for a moment after what you said about motive . . . but no, I know she's not capable of it. Only I'd like you to know that even if she had done such a thing it wouldn't make any difference to me. To my loving her, I mean. But you don't know her as I do.'

'In this case I don't need to, I have my own reasons for believing that someone else killed Winifred Paull, though as I said I'd rather not go into them now. So the first thing to do is to see about this charge against you, Mr Ryder.' He glanced at his watch. 'I'm afraid we've just about used up our time now, but we must talk again later.' He turned to his two colleagues. 'I'm going to ask for an adjournment,' he said. 'In the circumstances Carruthers will grant it . . . don't you think?'

'In the circumstances, I think he will,' Geoffrey agreed. 'If we're successful I'll arrange for Mr Ryder to be kept here until we've talked to him again, shall I?'

'That will be the best thing. It would be useless to tell you not to worry, Mr Ryder, but do your best to keep your head. We'll talk later.'

'And Carol?'

'We shall be seeing her later, too. Not that she can help us much at this stage, I imagine,' he added to his companions as they left the interview room and indicated to the warder outside that he could have his prisoner in charge again, 'but we must have a talk. There are a few loose ends.'

'Yes, I'm aware you've noticed them,' said Geoffrey, 'though I didn't think any conversation along those lines was advisable in our client's presence. But I admit I didn't expect —'

'You thought I'd take her guilt for granted too. When you, whom I know well to be one of the most sceptical of men, so obviously believe her innocent.'

'Is it as obvious as all that,' said Geoffrey, grinning suddenly.

'I should say it was pretty obvious, wouldn't you, Derek? But then you fell for her when you saw her before, didn't you?'

'Don't let Joan hear you say that,' Geoffrey implored him. 'And what's puzzling me at the moment is that belief in her innocence seems to have convinced you of Ryder's innocence too.'

'We'll talk about that later,' Maitland promised. 'Meanwhile give me five minutes, there's a good chap. I've got to put my thoughts in order before I make my request to old Carruthers.'

II

As Maitland had anticipated, Mr Justice Carruthers made no insuperable difficulties about his request for an adjournment, in view of the sudden demise of one of the prosecution witnesses. Geoffrey, who may or may not have been a scout in his boyhood but in any case made a practice of always being prepared for anything, had a detective constable standing by in case any corroboration of this statement should be needed, but in the event his evidence wasn't necessary. The judge looked inquiringly at Bruce Halloran, who was on his feet in a moment.

'My learned friend has already spoken to me of this distressing circumstance, my lord, and as he had not finished his cross-examination of Miss Paull —'

'Nor had you had the chance to re-examine,' said the judge slyly.

'— I felt it only proper to agree to his request.'

Carruthers looked consideringly at Counsel for the Defence for a moment, so that Antony was convinced that there was about to be some reference to 'one of Mr Maitland's fact-finding expeditions,' but evidently the judge resisted the temptation to indulge in a little mild humour at his expense. 'Since both of you are in agreement,' he said, 'I will adjourn the court until Monday next. I trust that will give both you gentlemen time to re-arrange your ideas.'

As the court emptied and Maitland made no attempt to follow the others, Geoffrey tugged at his sleeve. 'I thought you wanted to see our client again.'

'Yes I do, but you arranged that, didn't you? They won't take him away until we've seen him?'

'No, but how long do you intend to hang about here?'

'Just long enough to get a few things straight. For instance, you said she was lying face down on the rug with a gash on her temple and blood on her hair. Unless her hair was long enough to have fallen across her face, which it didn't look to be, though I admit it was difficult to tell with that stupid hat on, any bleeding would have been onto the carpet. And in any event Carol Ryder couldn't have seen — what was the phrase? — her hair matted with blood.'

'Winifred Paull didn't die immediately, and there *was* blood on the carpet, but there were other bloodstains too, from which it would seem that she was actually sitting down opposite the television set when she was hit.'

'And this piece of Eskimo carving you spoke of? Describe it, Geoffrey.'

'Sykes let me see it. It's a little difficult to tell you . . . the carving was crude, but the subject quite a complicated one. An Eskimo kneeling in a . . . kayak do you call them, or am I thinking of Red Indians? In a sort of canoe, anyway, and holding up a spear with which he seemed to intend to stab a bear. A polar bear, I suppose,' he added thoughtfully, 'but the whole thing was a sort of greenish colour.'

Antony grinned. 'What was the bear doing, waiting to be stabbed? Any self-respecting animal —'

'That's hardly important. The thing is, it was quite heavy, certainly heavy enough to do the damage. And spiky enough in places — the point of the spear, for instance — to account for the cut as well as the crushing of the skull.'

'And where had it been standing?'

'I don't know.'

'Was the flat as shiningly clean as it was when the S.I.S. people first examined it?'

'You mean there should have been a dust mark on one of the tables? I just don't know about that, Antony. What are you getting at?'

'That I very much doubt from what I saw of the lady whether Miss Paull's ideas of decorating her living quarters included anything quite so imaginative.'

'Well, if you insist on John Ryder's innocence the only person who could have told us that is dead.'

'Dr Gollnow may know.'

'But you can't talk to him, none of us can,' said Geoffrey, scandalised.

'You forget Carruthers said I might have him recalled.'

'To ask questions about this case, John Ryder's case. You'd have to go into a completely different matter —'

'Do *you* think they're unconnected?'

'What maggot have you got in your brain now?' asked Geoffrey, resigned.

'You were wondering why I had suddenly become convinced of both the Ryders' innocence of the crimes of which they are accused.'

'Of course, I'm wondering. And so is Derek,' he added, glancing at Stringer, who was waiting patiently for the argument to subside.

'Because I don't like coincidences,' Maitland told them. 'You may not have liked my handling of Winifred Paull yesterday afternoon —'

'I didn't,' said Geoffrey bluntly.

'No, you've made that quite obvious. However, you must admit I did succeed in upsetting her.'

'That's the whole point.'

'Yes, I know, but it also led me to certain irresistible conclusions. First, that it's my fault she was murdered —'

Stringer was moved to speak. 'That's ridiculous, Antony,

and you know it,' he said.

'No, I don't think so. Our case is that somebody borrowed John Ryder's identity, and if that's right it could only be someone who knew him well, who had access to his passport, in other words one of the three men he worked with in London. Each one of those three men had given his evidence and was sitting in the court while Miss Paull was in the witness-box. Don't you think he'd have been afraid, when he heard what I said and saw how she reacted to it, that she'd give him away when my questioning continued this morning?'

'I suppose you realise,' said Derek, 'that you're arguing in a circle. If Ryder is innocent and this man exists, then your argument is perfectly valid. But we still come back to that doubt, you know.'

'I don't like coincidences,' Antony repeated stubbornly. 'I can't believe in Carol Ryder deciding to kill Winifred Paull at that particular moment, when somebody else had a far better motive.'

'Only if . . . oh, let it go!' said Derek. 'It's no use arguing because I know perfectly well you're going your own way whatever I say. But what Geoffrey and I want to know is, what are you going to do about it?'

'I've been thinking about that, and I'm sorry to say, Derek, that the first thing is to do you out of a brief.'

'Do you think because I don't altogether agree with you —'

'No, nothing like that. Heaven and earth, we've worked together often enough when you thought — yes, and told me to my face — that I was stark, staring mad. What I meant was that neither of us is going to touch Carol Ryder's defence.'

'But you said —' Geoffrey began.

'I know what I said, I think she's innocent and that's why I want you to brief somebody from a completely different set of chambers. I can't see any way at all of dealing with the matter directly, so I want to talk to Sykes.'

116

There was a pause while his companions digested the statement. 'What will that do for you?' Geoffrey asked finally.

'How long will it take for the trial to come on?' He didn't wait for a reply. 'I'm like John Ryder, I don't want to see that baby born in prison.'

'Even so —'

'As defence counsel I can't talk to the investigating officer until the trial comes on and I can cross-examine him. Yes, I know I'm pointing out the obvious, but bear with me. You'd have details of the prosecution, but they wouldn't include the questions to which I want answers.'

'Do you think Sykes may get those answers for you?'

'I think he might be induced to try.'

'In any case, what help will that be if someone else is handling the defence?'

'It may confirm the impression I've got of the man who took our client's name in vain. If it does . . . don't you see, Geoffrey, it's the only chance we've got? It may not come off, but I've got to try.'

Horton and Stringer exchanged a glance. 'All right then,' said Geoffrey with a slight shrug. 'I suppose that means you don't want to see Mrs Ryder.'

'Now don't tell me that's something else I can't do.' Maitland's tone was becoming a little ragged. 'Whether she's under arrest or not I've every right to see her as a prospective witness in her husband's defence.'

'I'll arrange it. Meanwhile if you want to see Mr Ryder again —'   .

'Yes, I'll come now. You too, Derek?'

'Try to stop me.' But there was a good deal of incomprehension in the glance he exchanged with Geoffrey as Antony turned away, and a good deal of worry too.

III

Back in the interview room they found that John Ryder was, if anything, a little more jumpy than he had been before. 'A few more questions, Mr Ryder,' said Maitland as bracingly as he could.

'Can't they wait until you've done something for Carol?'

'Will you believe me if I assure you that you can best help your wife by doing your utmost to clear your own name?'

Ryder looked at him for a long moment. 'I'm in your hands, Mr Maitland,' he said at last, and wondered at Antony's quick frown.

'It won't take long,' Maitland assured him. 'And if it will make you happier I'll begin with a question that does have a bearing on your wife's predicament. Are you familiar with Eskimo carvings?'

'I know them when I see them.'

'You don't own anything of the sort yourself?'

'We certainly don't.'

'That's good. And there's nothing of the kind in your sister's flat.'

'No. There are some souvenirs of their travels, but Henry's work has usually taken him south.'

'Have you seen anything of the sort in any of your colleagues' homes? The men in the London office, I mean.'

'I haven't, but surely —'

'Don't start wondering what's behind my questions, Mr Ryder. I'm not sure myself yet. Now, one or two points from the evidence yesterday afternoon.'

'Yes, that was a bit of a facer, wasn't it?' If there had been room for amusement in John Ryder at the moment Antony would have said that he appreciated some humour in the situation. 'To see ourselves as others see us,' he said. 'It isn't given to everyone, but I don't know that I'm grateful for the opportunity.'

'You told us already why you preferred to do your entertaining away from home, away from your sister's home, that is. When you spent the evening with Mr Walters were you in the habit of leaving him fairly early?'

'Yes, he was quite right about that. He's an older man, we hadn't a great deal in common. But he's quite wrong —'

'You're getting ahead of me, Mr Ryder. I was just going to ask you whether you recall dining with him at Ricardo's.'

'Several times, I daresay. It was one of those places I sometimes took people more than once, but I don't believe I was ever there alone.'

'Do you remember the occasion Mr Walters mentioned, when you spoke to somebody as you were leaving?'

'I might have been speaking to Ricardo, I've been there often enough for him to know me by sight and greet me when he sees me.'

'Would you say he's anything like Dr Gollnow in appearance?'

'No, I wouldn't, but I daresay . . . well I have to admit, Mr Maitland, a description of one of them might fit the other, though if they were standing side by side you wouldn't take them for twins.'

'I see. And what about "getting home to the little woman"?'

'If I said anything of the kind I was referring to the end of the week when I'd go home to Carol, but I'm quite sure I never used that particular rather ghastly phrase.'

'But you wouldn't think it altogether out of character for Mr Walters to do so?'

'Oh no, it's the sort of thing he *would* say, I suppose,' — again there was the slight quirk of the lips, before he remembered the seriousness of the present situation — 'that's the sort of thing that made me rather anxious to get away from him in the evening.'

'Yes, I can see it would be. Let's go on to your other friends then.'

'Jane Braithwaite's rather a dear, isn't she? It was rather

mean of the prosecutor to twist what she said around like that. I do like women, but not quite in the way he implied. Some women, in the same way that I like some men. Others I simply can't stand.'

'I don't think you need worry about what Mrs Braithwaite said too much, but we'll come back to that in a moment. Mr Braithwaite —'

'Yes, I think I did say once that it would be a good idea if everybody in the world exchanged technical information freely. I didn't quite mean it, though. It was one of those remarks one tosses up hoping to get an argument going. I think Ernest should have realised that more clearly than he did.'

'And Mr Gibbon's remark about your complaining about being short of money, but still throwing it around freely?'

'Oh that! We all talk about being hard-up; I've told you how it was with Carol and me. We'd enough, but not enough to throw around. When it came to these London trips, I was on a fixed expense allowance which took into consideration the fact that in the ordinary way, I'd have had to pay hotel bills. It's one thing to be frugal at home, but when you're away by yourself . . . I couldn't see any harm in spending it that way.'

'That brings us to the last point, Mr Ryder. Perhaps the most important one. Mrs Gibbon says she saw you at Ricardo's with Miss Paull one evening.'

Ryder frowned. 'That's the one thing I don't understand and I can't explain,' he said. 'Edith has no quarrel with me, though I can't say I'm as fond of her as I am of Jane, so I can't see why she should make such a thing up. But I've never been to Ricardo's alone with a woman, I can assure you of that. I've taken Mr Walters there, and I've taken Ernest and Jane and William and Edith there too, sometimes all together, and sometimes just two of them. I'm sure if you ask —'

'Mr Horton already has that in hand. That's all I need worry you with now, Mr Ryder, and I shall see you again in court on Monday morning. Before we go I think I'd better explain to you that Mr Stringer and I have decided after all not to accept the briefs in your wife's defence. No, wait just a moment! That's not because we don't believe your story, but because we do,' he said firmly, and only realised afterwards that he should have been speaking for himself alone. 'If you'll just listen I'll try to explain it to you . . .'

IV

The rest of the interview was not without its distressing side. When it was over at last Derek left them to go back to chambers and Geoffrey sought out a telephone; after which he and Antony went to lunch before going out to Holloway Prison where Caroline Ryder was now being held.

Caroline was not very tall. She had dark hair that curled tightly about her head, and hazel eyes that — Maitland found after a few moments converse — were capable of giving a very direct, assessing look. In the ordinary way he thought her figure would quite accurately be described as slight. Now, already, she was only too obviously pregnant, an uncomfortable reminder that the situation might be considered as more than usually urgent. Not surprisingly she was very pale, but she had herself well in hand.

Antony, who felt that a visit to a woman's prison was just about the worst thing that he could be asked to do, several degrees worse even than a similar vist to one of his male clients, waited patiently while Geoffrey performed the introductions. She turned to him eagerly then. 'You're trying to help John,' she said. And then, dividing the question equally between them, 'How is he?'

It was Geoffrey who took it upon himself to reply. 'Rather more worried about you than he is about himself at the moment. But I think first of all I should explain Mr Maitland's position.'

'He's a barrister, isn't he? Though I must say I'd never

have recognised him without his wig. But I thought his being here must mean he was going to represent me too.'

'Not exactly that. You see —'

'It's important for us to get the distinction clear, Mrs Ryder.' Maitland thought it was time he took a hand. 'For reasons of — of legal etiquette, which I won't trouble you with at the moment, it's important that I should have a free hand in defending your husband.'

'I don't understand.'

'No, I was afraid you wouldn't.' He smiled at her. 'Please believe me, I'm trying to do the best thing for both of you. Will you take my word for it?'

'Yes, of course.' Her eyes were fixed questioningly on his face, but what she saw there must have satisfied her. There was hesitation in her tone, but no real doubt. 'But that still leaves me wondering why, in that case, you wanted to see me.'

'Officially, as a possible witness in your husband's defence.'

'But Mr Horton said —'

'Yes, I know, and what he told you still applies. I admit he offered me a brief in your case too, but that would tie my hands over certain actions I wish to take, and quite frankly we can't afford it.'

'Does that mean you really think you can do something for John?'

'I don't know,' he replied honestly. 'I only know I want to, and if I can help him I shall be helping you at the same time. Only you mustn't count on anything.'

It was her turn to smile. 'Very well, Mr Maitland,' she said, and sat down at the end of the table with a fair degree of composure. 'What do you want to know?'

'First, I want you to answer a question for me and then forget I ever asked it. Before I decided how best to deal with this, I mean before I decided it would be inadvisable for me to act for you, Mr Horton told me the full story of what happened last night as you had told it to him. Have you had

122

any cause to reconsider any part of that statement?'

That brought a frown. 'If you mean did I kill that woman, no I didn't.' And then, as though suddenly enlightened, 'That's what you meant, isn't it? How stupid of me not to have realised it. You don't believe me about that, and that's why —'

'Please, Mrs Ryder, I meant what I said to you earlier, no more and no less. But part of my argument in your husband's favour . . . let's leave it there, shall we? Will you trust me so far?'

Again there was that long, considering look. 'Yes, of course I will,' she said.

'Then we can go on from there. As you know, Mr Horton has told me that you were ready to give evidence on behalf of your husband if we had thought it advisable. What did you think you could say to help him?'

'I don't quite know,' she told him helplessly. 'Only I thought . . . if only I could make people understand the kind of man John is, that he would never under any circumstances have done a thing like that —'

'Like what, Mrs Ryder?'

'Why . . . betray everything he believed in.'

'We'll come back to that in a moment. Treachery — or rather, if I must be accurate Geoffrey, an offence under the Official Secrets Act — though the only thing mentioned in the indictment isn't all he's being accused of.'

Again she paused to think that out. 'I suppose you mean that the fact that he's said to have been leading a double life might count against him when the jury is considering the charge. All I can tell you is, that's quite impossible too.'

'I wonder if Mr Horton has explained to you that Mr Ryder was very doubtful whether you believed that he'd been faithful to you.'

'Yes, he told me, and I begged him to make John understand.'

'I know he did his best about that. I think perhaps now —'

She gave a sudden gasp and interrupted him without

123

ceremony. 'You're not going to tell me he believes *I* killed that woman?' she said.

'No, I'm quite sure he doesn't.' Please God there'd be an opportunity later for these two to sort out their relationship without any interference from outside. 'But I do wonder, Mrs Ryder, how you arrived at those very positive assertions you made. I can very well understand it would be difficult to admit to yourself that your husband had married bigamously only six months after he went through a wedding ceremony with you, and from that denial it would follow that he wasn't the John Ryder who acted as a go-between between Dennis Nesbit and Dr Boris Gollnow.'

She smiled a little, though very faintly, a mere acknowledgement of the point he had made. 'You're quite right, of course. If I believed either allegation *that* might well have been the most important one to me. But you can't live with a person for three years without getting to know them through and through.'

'Mr Ryder told us, however, that there'd been some disagreement between you the last time he came to town. That you'd accused him of enjoying the time he spent away from you.'

'Yes, that's quite true. I don't know what came over me.'

'Perhaps it would be as well if you told us about your association with your husband from the beginning.'

'We knew each other as children. Our families were friends, though the Ryders lived in Wolverhampton and I lived with my parents in Bloxwich. They're all dead now, John's parents and mine, and I don't know whether to be glad or sorry. I wouldn't have put them through all this for anything, but I have to admit I'm weak enough to wish that they were still around. I wouldn't want Mother or my father either, coming to a place like this, but it would be an awfully comforting thing to have a shoulder to cry on.'

'I'm afraid', said Antony, smiling at her, 'you'll have to make do with Mr Horton. As I explained, I shan't be coming here again. But to get back to this childhood friendship —'

'I had no brothers or sisters, and John had just Edwina who is awfully nice but quite a bit older. Perhaps that's what brought us together in spite of our difference in age, which is nothing now, but of course when we were children it seemed enormous.' She closed her eyes for a moment, perhaps so that she could forget the dingy room, and concentrate on more pleasant things. 'I think it was most fun when the Ryders came to visit us. John wasn't used to the country, so there were things I could show him which made me feel quite important, but after a while he began to devise all sorts of games, things to do, that I'd never have thought of in a hundred years. That was nice too. In town it wasn't quite so much fun, we were neither of us allowed to go to the pictures alone, and there were all kinds of taboos about where we should go. Still we did a lot of talking.'

'What was John like then?'

She gave him a look in which for the moment amusement seemed to predominate. 'I'm his wife, you know, and I love him,' she said.

'Still, you're going to try to justify those opinions of yours, aren't you?'

'Yes, I suppose I must. He was . . . well, I have to admit he was a little reckless, always dragging me into mischief I'd never have thought of for myself.' Maitland felt Horton's eyes on him, but ignored the look and hoped that Carol Ryder had done so too. 'But what I think's important about that is that if there was any trouble he never tried to make excuses. He was absolutely truthful, sometimes uncomfortably so.'

'And besides that?'

'I thought him terribly clever, and now I know I was right. But at that time I knew nothing about most of the things he was interested in. I used to tag along blindly and agree with everything he said. But you see, Mr Maitland, this only went on until his parents died, just about the time he was due to go to his public school. After that he went to live with some older cousins, not local people, and we lost touch for years.'

'Had he been a boarder at his prep school?'

'Yes, but we still saw each other regularly during the holidays.'

'When did you meet again?'

'Not until about four years ago. He was working at Wycherley's, and because Wolverhampton was no longer home to him, and hadn't been for some time, I think he must have been rather lonely.'

'Did he tell you that?'

'Not in so many words. I suppose it was how I explained to myself the fact that he came over to Bloxwich one day. My parents were still alive — they died in a car crash a year after we were married — and we were living in the same place, and one Saturday afternoon he turned up on the doorstep.'

'And you took up where you left off?'

'More or less.'

'Let me see if I've got this straight. You husband is about thirty now —'

'Thirty and three months,' she told him precisely.

'And you're . . . how much younger, Mrs Ryder?'

'Three years.'

'So at that time you were twenty-three to his twenty-six. If I may be impertinent, Mrs Ryder, how did it come that an attractive girl like you was still unmarried?'

'I just was, that's all.'

'No suitors?'

'One or two, but nobody I took seriously.'

'Not dedicated to your career?'

'Certainly not that.' She broke off there, and again seemed to be weighing him up. 'What are you thinking?' she demanded after a moment.

'That perhaps you'd never quite forgotten your childhood friend, and you think that if you tell us that —'

'You're quite right, you'll just think I'm besotted with

him, and would say anything to defend him.'

'As a matter of fact, Mrs Ryder, you're wrong about that. You've told us your husband has a truthful nature, but I'd be willing to bet the same description could be applied to you.'

'I don't know, I think there are things I would lie about. But I'm not lying about this.'

It was Maitland's turn to hesitate. 'Your husband told me he was in my hands,' he said after a while, unwillingly. 'Now I'm going to have to ask you to trust me too.'

'Very well. You're quite right, I'd always remembered John.'

'And seemingly he had remembered you. Why no correspondence?'

'I did write to him a couple of times but got no reply. But you must remember, Mr Maitland, that we'd looked on each other practically as brother and sister, and there comes a time in a boy's life — at least so it seems to me — when he's rather ashamed of having a sister. I don't expect John felt like that by the time he left school, but we'd lost touch by then and it would have been difficult to take up the acquaintance again through correspondence.'

'That's a very acute observation, Mrs Ryder, and I think you're probably right. Anyway, what happened at this reunion of yours?'

'He stayed to tea, not exactly romantic, but after that we saw each other regularly. I was working in Wolverhampton, so it was quite easy during the week, and after a month or so he spent most of his weekends with us. And I think we were in love almost from the first.'

'During that period of your courtship did he tell you anything about his friends before he met you again?'

'He had some friends at the office, of course, but I think you mean women friends, don't you? As a matter of fact he didn't, and of course I never asked because really if he'd a list as long as Leporello's it wouldn't have been any of my business. But I did gather once when he took me to visit the cousins he'd lived with . . . well, it was Mrs Nash who was a cousin of his mother's, though very much older. She told me she was so relieved that John had met me because he'd never had a taste for casual encounters.'

'I see. And after a year you were married?'

'Yes, and we arranged that I should go on with my job so that we could save up to have a really good down payment on a house before we started a family. I hated it when he was away, of course, and particularly after my parents died, but it wasn't until I was pregnant that I began, quite unreasonably, to resent it a little.'

'Did he tell you about his life during those weeks in London?'

'Yes, naturally. He stayed at his sister's, I'm sure you know that, and he talked about the people he met at the office, but I don't think he had time really to make any other friends. He used to go up on Sunday evening, because of putting in a full day at the office on Monday, but he nearly always came home on Friday night.'

'Nearly always, Mrs Ryder?'

'There were just a few occasions when he stayed over, when there were jobs he wanted to finish. But it didn't happen very often.'

'Do you keep any sort of a diary. Could you identify the weekends he stayed a day longer?'

'No, I'm afraid not.'

'Did you have any communication with him during these absences?'

'He used to phone me every evening.'

'You never phoned him at his sister's flat?'

'Not regularly, because he always dined out. So it was easier for him to call me when he got in.'

'But you did call sometimes?'

'Once or twice, when I had something special to tell him, but I always managed to choose the wrong time, so I saw then that he'd been sensible to suggest the other arrangement.'

Again Antony was conscious of Geoffrey's restless movement. 'Now when Mr Ryder came home,' he said, 'what was the procedure? Did you unpack for him?'

'Yes, usually.'

'Sent his clothes to the laundry, his suits to the cleaners, that sort of thing?'

'Exactly that sort of thing.'

'So I suppose you went through the pockets of his suits first — I know my wife always does — in case he'd left anything there.'

'If you're thinking I might have found something incriminating, you're quite mistaken, Mr Maitland. There was never anything to make me think he wasn't living exactly as he said.'

'Thank you, yes, that was my point. But there could be another one too. According to the — the other Mrs Ryder they usually ate at home. If you found receipts for restaurant meals for instance —'

'I wouldn't though. He kept those in his wallet because they had to go in with his expenses.'

'In spite of his having a fixed allowance.'

'Actually, I don't think he need have submitted them. Only he had this thing about everything being above board, didn't want to conceal the fact that he hadn't any hotel bills. And he had the idea that everything he received from the firm for expenses could only be used while he was away, not on any account at home. So you see, I wouldn't have seen them.'

'No, of course you wouldn't. Why on earth didn't we think of that before? Another job for you, Geoffrey, get Mr Ryder's expense accounts at Wycherley's checked out.' But Horton was writing already.

'That should have been obvious,' he added apologetically.

'Well, I didn't think of it either,' Maitland pointed out.

'No, but you came into the affair rather late in the day. I'll tell you what it is,' said Geoffrey, 'I'm getting too used to letting you do my thinking for me. Not a good thing.'

'Well there's no need to be as elliptical about it as Vera would be,' said Antony. And did not add what was in his mind, that if Geoffrey had agreed with him wholeheartedly in the conclusions he had reached since Winifred Paull's death the solicitor would in all likelihood have thought of that line of questioning himself.

'Have I really said something that might help?' asked Carol eagerly.

'A small thing, such a small thing. Yes, I believe you have,' said Maitland smiling at her. 'But it leads to another question, you know. Were there any phone calls for John while he was at home that he may have been mysterious or secretive about?'

'No. If he took the call he might sometimes just say it was business, but there were never any strange female voices asking for him when I lifted the receiver, if that's what you mean.'

'Nothing at all that could be construed as evidence of this double life he was supposed to have been living?'

'Nothing at all.'

'And as to a more serious matter, there's been some mention of his favouring freedom of scientific information throughout the world.'

'I heard that. Well, he wants peace, don't we all? And I think he feels that would act rather like everyone having nuclear weapons, so that no one dare use them.'

That wasn't exactly the explanation that Ryder had given, but there might be elements of truth in both. Maitland chose to take up the lesser point. 'But pacifism, however commendable in itself, has led people into strange actions in the past.'

'You mean the people who say everything we do is all wrong, and everything the Russians do is all right,' said Carol rather scornfully. 'I do assure you, Mr Maitland, you must have realised this if you've talked to him, John isn't in any way a fanatic. He's just an ordinary Englishman with a love for his country which he's never mentioned, of course, — he'd die rather — but which is there just the same.'

'Thank you, Mrs Ryder. We'll leave it there then.' Maitland, whose instinct for movement had been kept in check with difficulty for the last ten minutes pushed his chair back and got to his feet. 'You've been very helpful and very patient.'

'I can't help wishing you were going to represent me too,' she told him.

'I'm afraid that's impossible. Mr Horton will explain to you better than I can,' he added unfairly. 'He'll be coming to see you again before long, when he's arranged for counsel. Meanwhile I expect he'd like a word with you before we go. I'll wait for you outside, Geoffrey.'

V

For some reason, probably because he sensed that his friend's mind was not altogether at ease, Geoffrey showed no signs of wishing to thrash over what they had learned on the way back to town, and allowed Antony to go back to chambers alone without further discussion. It was a relief to Antony to find that his uncle was in conference. Any delay in discussing what had happened would certainly have been unpopular, but he wanted a little time to himself to put his ideas in order. Willett took one knowledgeable look at him as he went in, and went back into the clerk's office to instruct Hill quite firmly that Mr Maitland mustn't be disturbed on any account, either by phone calls or visitors. By the time Sir Nicholas made his way down the corridor to his nephew's rooms an hour and a half later it was already growing dark.

'Good heavens, Antony, what on earth are you doing sitting in the dark?' Sir Nicholas demanded, flicking the switch by the door as he spoke. It was a rather gloomy room even on the sunniest day, and for a moment the older man stood in the doorway looking around him distastefully. 'If you're still brooding about your last witness —'

'I'm considering a course of action, Uncle Nick, and I'd like to talk to you about it.'

'I'm open to being talked to,' said Sir Nicholas carefully, 'at this time of year.'

'Yes, I know. At least, I hope you are.'

'You're burbling, Antony. If you've something to say, say it, only for heaven's sake come to my room first and let's leave this dismal place behind.'

'You wouldn't let Jenny re-paint it,' Antony pointed out, following him. 'And I think on the whole, Uncle Nick,' he added, as they went in to the much more luxurious room which Sir Nicholas, as head of chambers, occupied, 'that it would be better if we had the whole thing out tonight. I don't want to interfere with either Jenny or Vera's dinner arrangments, and this may take some time.'

'In that case, let us by all means go home. I take it', said Sir Nicholas, reaching up a hand for his overcoat, 'that you're contemplating some lunacy.'

'It all depends how you look at it. I admit that even Derek was moved to argue with the conclusions I've drawn from what's happened.'

'For which no doubt I should be grateful to him. Anyway, Antony, if you think it's best, we'll talk after dinner. No doubt Vera will have something useful to add to the discussion.'

'Yes, but —'

Sir Nicholas gave him one of his more penetrating looks. 'You're not suggesting that we should exclude her from our discussion?' he said.

'Not exactly.'

'Come, my dear boy,' said Sir Nicholas, almost as grimly as his wife might have done, 'it must be one thing or the other.'

'Uncle Nick you know how I value Vera, I don't want to keep her from knowing what's going on. but the thing is, with your permission, I was going to ask Sykes to join us a little later in the evening, and he doesn't know Vera as we do. He may be more willing to do what I ask if it's just the two of us.'

'I see,' said Sir Nicholas slowly. 'Or do I? I'm to be there to lend some semblance of propriety to your request, but — '

'That's it exactly. Don't you see, Uncle Nick, it's going to de damned difficult anyway?'

'In any case you're not in a position to talk to Chief Inspector Sykes.'

'He has nothing to do with the prosecution in John Ryder's case.'

'That is undoubtedly true. But let me remind you, Antony, the police, and specifically Chief Inspector Sykes, are involved in Winifred Paull's death; and though you may have every intention of keeping from contentious matters, I feel that your action in talking to him at all may, to say the least, be open to misinterpretation. And in view of Chief Superintendent Briggs's attitude towards you —'

'I know perfectly well that Briggs has been gunning for me for years,' said Antony, causing a pained expression to cross his uncle's face, 'but I've no intention of standing still long enough for him to get a good shot. In any case, Uncle Nick, you're doing exactly what you always warn me against, jumping to conclusions.'

'Indeed?'

'You're assuming — aren't you? — that I'm going to accept a brief to defend Caroline Ryder.'

'Is that not your intention?'

'No, of course not. I quite see I couldn't talk to Sykes if I did. Geoffrey's looking for somebody else, not connected with these chambers, but to be honest with you I'm hoping the case will never come to trial.'

'That seems rather unlikely in the circumstances as I have heard them.'

'It's a long story, Uncle Nick —'

'And we shall both be better for food and drink,' said Sir Nicholas, suddenly brisk. 'We'll go home now and you can bring Jenny down after dinner. Unless Sykes agrees to come . . . what time were you thinking of asking him for, by the way?'

'I thought nine-thirty or thereabouts. He'll be working late, with not much more than twenty-four hours passed since the murder, and I think he'll be curious enough to want to know what I have to say.'

'You may be right. And in any event, as I was saying, when and if Chief Inspector Sykes arrives we'll see him alone. You can have the pleasure of explaining to Jenny, as I will to Vera, your reasons for wanting this arrangement. And if they don't accept them,' he added, ushering Antony before him out of the room, 'may the Lord have mercy on both our souls.'

VI

Jenny took that particular explanation calmly, and Antony was pretty sure Vera would accept it equally well. They went downstairs therefore as soon as they judged that the slightly ceremonious repast upon which Gibbs insisted would be over, and found Sir Nicholas and his wife, as they had expected, drinking coffee by the fire in the study. 'I hope you've got enough coal left,' said Antony, after he had greeted Vera with the slight formality he still affected with her. 'We've enough for two or three weeks, but Jenny says —'

'Never mind the aftermath of the coal strike,' Vera adjured him. 'Gather this is important.'

Antony, sinking down beside Jenny on the sofa, thought about that for a moment. 'Its importance depends upon two things,' he said then. 'One, whether *I'm* right about the Ryders, or two, if I *am* right, can I do anything about it.'

'What precisely,' asked Sir Nicholas, 'is it that you want

to do?'

'I want to clear John Ryder, and in doing so expose Winifred Paull's killer. Which will automatically get Caroline Ryder off the hook,' he added, as though any of his listeners might be unsure of what he meant.

'You were in some doubt about Ryder's innocence or guilt last time we talked,' Vera pointed out.

'Yes, of course I was, but don't you see this murder changed everything?'

'I see it's resulted in his wife's arrest. And that you're feeling sorry for the pair of them,' she added, almost as if it was an accusation.

'If you mean I'm thinking that neither of them is guilty as charged because of some sentimental clap-trap, you're wrong,' Antony retorted. 'It isn't pleasant to think of the child being born in prison, but I assure you that's not influencing me.'

'You can't expect them to understand it', said Jenny, 'until you explain it to them.'

'From which I take it, my dear, that he has talked you over to his point of view,' said Sir Nicholas.

'Yes, of course, Uncle Nick. He says Geoffrey and Derek don't agree with him, but *I* think the argument is very sound,' said Jenny firmly.

'In that case I think we had better hear it.'

It was the same argument he had put forward to his colleagues earlier in the day, perhaps expressed with a little more clarity because of the time he had had to think it out. When he had finished, neither of his listeners spoke for a moment.

'Can't think what you expect Chief Inspector Sykes to do about it,' said Vera at last.

'Now I thought your first idea would be to commend my discretion,' said Antony. At the best of times he hated explanations, and at the moment his main feeling was one of relief that this one was at least in part behind him.

'If you mean for not accepting a brief to defend Caroline

135

Ryder, nothing else you could do,' said Vera. 'Not if you want to talk to Sykes. But I don't see —'

'That's because you haven't had quite so much time for reflection as I have, my dear,' Sir Nicholas assured her. At that moment they heard Gibbs's footsteps going heavily down the hall, though they had all been too engrossed in what was being said to hear the front-door bell.

Antony glanced quickly at his watch. 'That's Sykes now,' he asserted, 'dead on time. Vera, did Uncle Nick explain —?'

'He did, and if you want me to commend your discretion, as you put it, I'll do so for that,' Vera assured him, getting rather heavily to her feet. 'Come along, Jenny,' she added. 'You won't refuse me refuge for a while.'

If the two were still in sight when he was admitted, Chief Inspector Sykes made no comment on the fact to Antony when he came in. He was a squarish-built man, a countryman rather than a townsman from his appearance, and in all the years he had lived in London his north country accent had never forsaken him. He and Maitland were old friends — and that was the right word, Antony thought, even though at times they had also been adversaries. Of late years a mutual regard had brought them closer to each other, and each one regarded himself as in some way indebted to the other, while neither was of a nature to take such an obligation — real or imagined — lightly.

The first item of business was the detective's careful inquiries as to their well-being and that of the other members of the family. He had a strong sense of propriety, and any omission of this rite would have made Antony extremely nervous. At last, however, reassurance on all points had been given, and Mrs Sykes too, they learned, was in excellent health.

'Well now, Mr Maitland,' said the visitor, settling himself comfortably in the chair that was now generally occupied by Vera, and accepting with a murmur of thanks Sir Nicholas's offer of cognac, 'it's very pleasant to see you

136

and Sir Nicholas again, but your summons sounded urgent and for the life of me I can't think what business we have together at the moment.'

'Would you like to tell him, Uncle Nick?'

'No, no, my boy, it's your affair. Besides,' he added — and his nephew for one had no doubt of the exact meaning that lay behind the words — 'I'm quite sure you will explain yourself to the Chief Inspector much more eloquently than I could.'

No help for it then. 'The thing is,' said Antony ingenuously, 'I think I can be of some help to you, Chief Inspector.'

It wasn't to be expected that the detective would take a remark like that lying down, particularly from someone he knew so well. 'Mr Maitland,' he asked anxiously, 'are you sure you're feeling quite well?'

Antony grinned at him. Perhaps this wasn't going to go so badly after all. 'Don't you start,' he implored. 'I know Briggs thinks I'd stoop to anything.'

'No, no, Mr Maitland, you know better than that. I've never complained of anything beyond the fact that you're not always willing to be perfectly open with me. No doubt for the best of reasons,' he added thoughtfully. 'Or what seem to you the best of reasons.'

'For the best of reasons,' Antony insisted. 'However, this time the boot's on the other leg.' For once he hardly noticed Sir Nicholas's anguished look. 'To a certain extent I'm able and willing to be perfectly open with you, and I think I can — shall we say? — open a few avenues in the matter of Winifred Paull's murder for you to explore.'

'I was under the impression that an arrest had already been made.'

'Yes, I know, but —'

'Let me ask you one thing, Mr Maitland. Are you representing Caroline Ryder?'

'My dear Chief Inspector! Should I be talking to you now if I were?'

'Then am I to take it that you have some further evidence in the matter?'

'On the contrary, that is if you mean further evidence against her. Look, I think you made a mistake but, if my opinion's of any value I don't see what else you could have done in the circumstances. But there could be another way of looking at the matter, and unless I tell you about it, it's something you couldn't possibly know.'

'Then it's certainly my duty to listen to you. I wonder, Sir Nicholas —'

'If you mean, does my uncle agree with me about this, I don't know,' Antony admitted frankly, forestalling Sir Nicholas's reply. 'But I'm quite sure he's with me so far as to say that if there's any doubt at all it should be examined.'

Sykes looked inquiringly at the older man. 'That, certainly,' said Sir Nicholas. 'There is also, if Antony will forgive my saying so, the matter of my own peace of mind. I may not exactly be happier when I know what he is about, but I certainly feel it expedient to have that information.'

'Yes, I see your point,' said Sykes seriously. 'Very well, Mr Maitland. Am I to take it that all this has something to do with your defence of John Ryder?'

'Yes, it has.' Maitland would have strenuously denied any suggestion that he was an eloquent advocate, but a simple statement of facts was another matter, and now all his facility in that direction seemed to have deserted him too. 'I have to admit that I accepted the brief mainly to oblige Geoffrey Horton, and even when I began to have doubts of my client's guilt I was still by no means certain until I had had a chance to think over what happened last night.'

'You mean the murder of Winifred Paull?'

'Yes, of course I do. Surely you will have heard that she collapsed in the middle of my cross-examination of her. You can take it from me, Chief Inspector, that what she had told me would in no way have helped John Ryder's case, nor did I expect any better fortune this morning if she had still been

138

alive. But it may well have seemed to someone less familiar with the ways of juries that there was a fairly good chance of her breaking down and telling me the truth.'

'The truth?' Sykes echoed, so that for a moment Antony thought he was going to continue rhetorically, *'What is truth?'*

'I can understand your doubts, but don't you think there was too much coincidence about? Never mind my reasons for thinking John Ryder innocent, they're based merely on my impression of him and the other witnesses, and in no way amount to proof. But just grant for a moment, for the sake of argument, that I'm right about that.'

'I have to point out that there are a good many difficulties in the way, so far as I have followed the case.'

'Two witnesses who positively identify him — that's the main thing, isn't it?'

'And the passport that was found, not in the flat he said he occupied in London, but in the one he shared with Winifred Paull. Who believed herself to be married to him.'

'Then let us take our suppositions one step further. Suppose the two people who identified him were lying.'

'Can you suggest any reason why they should?'

'Very easily, though I'm afraid it's still conjecture, and I doubt if my uncle will accept it. In the case of Dr Gollnow, he's asking for political asylum. That may be perfectly genuine, or it may be because he has ambitions to become a double agent. I don't pretend to know, but in either case it's important to him to be accepted. He has named two men, Dennis Nesbit, correctly as it turns out, and John Ryder, whom he does not see immediately. By the time he does see my client, Miss Paull, whom he knew as Mrs Ryder, has already identified him as her husband. Gollnow might feel it expedient to agree with her, that her word would be more likely to be believed than his . . . don't you think? After all, so far as the authorities know, she's a perfectly respectable housewife.'

'As you say, Mr Maitland . . . conjecture.'

'You needn't remind me. Let's come to Miss Paull then, which is rather simpler. If she knew what was going on, and it's hard to see how she could have failed to do so, though she denies it, for her it is simply a matter of protecting the man who assumed John Ryder's identity.'

'You're telling me that someone deliberately built up a second life for your client, for the real John Ryder, just in case any questions arose in the future.'

'Do you find that so very hard to believe? It seems perfectly logical to me, and that's why our man didn't bolt when he learned of Gollnow's defection; even if he'd said he'd never seen John Ryder before, he still didn't know the fake John Ryder's name.'

'In court —'

'Don't you see, there'd have been no trial if Gollnow had denied knowing my client. And once the identification had been made the other man must have felt perfectly safe. He was never worried about Winifred Paull, who thought she was married to him whether she was or not; he must have made an opportunity quite early in the game for her to see Ryder and be able to identify him if things went wrong.'

Chief Inspector Sykes glanced at Sir Nicholas, and shook his head slightly. 'If I grant its logic,' he said, turning back to Antony, 'there would still be certain difficulties in carrying out the plan.'

'Exactly, but those very difficulties may be of the greatest help to us. John Ryder — I'm talking of my client now, the John Ryder who lives in Wolverhampton and spends one week in three in London, and is married to Caroline Ryder — '

'Who is herself at present under arrest for murder,' Sykes reminded him.

'Never mind that for the moment. John Ryder, I say, didn't have many friends in London, just the three men who worked in the office where he had a desk when he was in town. And the wives of the two of them who were married as well, but it's the men I'm concerned with. He kept his passport in his briefcase, and hadn't had occasion to look for it for some time. When he was in London the briefcase went to the office with him. Don't you think one of those three men could have had an opportunity of removing it?'

'Could have, Mr Maitland, not necessarily did.'

'Oh, I admit that, but for the moment we're assuming Ryder's innocence . . . remember? If somebody deliberately built up this second life for him it must have been someone who knew him well, who knew his circumstances and the details of his visits to London. Again, those three men fill the bill. And each of them gave evidence today, and was sitting in court while Winifred Paull was in the witness-box. Any of them might have made the mistake I mentioned to you just now, and killed her to save his own skin.'

'Even so —'

'Won't you even admit that it's rather a coincidence that Winifred Paull should be murdered just when she might be thought to be in difficulties with her evidence?'

'I grant you that much, Mr Maitland.' Sykes sounded doubtful. 'But the question still remains, what do you want me to do about it?'

'Co-operate,' said Antony simply. '*I* can't approach them, you must see that. They're prosecution witnesses in a case in which I'm involved.'

'For that matter, neither can I,' Sykes pointed out. 'I know of nothing to connect any one of them with Winifred Paull.'

'But you could find out something about them and their habits without ever approaching them. You could find out where they were last night for instance.'

'I could,' said Sykes more doubtfully than ever.

'And another thing, you could get photographs of them and find out if any of them were ever seen at Brinkley Court. No one ever seems to have noticed anyone except Winifred Paull going in or out of the apartment that was taken in John Ryder's name, but people see one another in the lift, there might be something there.'

141

'Do you know what you're asking me, Mr Maitland?'

'Yes, I do.'

'To do all this unofficially, as it were?'

'Briggs is your superior officer, and Briggs wouldn't approve. But I think you've sufficient ingenuity to ensure that he need never know a thing about it.'

'We've been friends for a long time —'

'That isn't why I'm asking you. I wouldn't ask you to take it on if I was the only one to benefit. In fact, I can only answer you by sounding thoroughly corny. In the interests of justice —'

'Yes, I take your point. If there's any chance that we're wrong about Mrs Ryder . . . you'd better give me particulars of these three men.'

'I've got their names and addresses written down,' said Antony, fumbling in his pocket. 'I printed them,' he added, 'so as to be sure they were readable.'

'And have you no favourite among them?'

This time Antony's pause was so long that Sykes became visibly restless, a thing very unlike him. 'Each one of them had something to say against John Ryder,' Maitland said at last, 'and Edith Gibbon — look at the list, she's William Gibbon's wife — had quite a circumstantial story about seeing him with someone whom she later recognised as Winifred Paull. But I think, if you don't mind, we'll leave it there. Don't you understand, Sykes,' he added, almost in desperation, after another pause, 'I only want to be sure?'

'And then what?'

'I don't know. How can I know at this stage?'

'I think you've got some idea in your head,' said Sykes shrewdly, 'but I won't press you just now. Is there anything else you want to know?' From anyone else the question might have sounded like sarcasm, but that wasn't the detective's way.

'Yes, two things. This chap who caught Caroline Ryder, as he thought red-handed, what about him?'

'You're thinking he seems to be a little less uninterested

in other people's affairs than the other tenants in the building,' said Sykes. 'Yes, I think that's true, but you must remember he heard a woman cry out. That may have been the murdered woman —'

'Or it may have been Caroline Ryder, shocked by her discovery.'

'So it may,' agreed Sykes noncommittally. 'However, I don't think you need worry about the neighbour, he only moved in at the beginning of the month, so I'm afraid he's not going to be much help to us.'

'No, I can see that. The other thing is the weapon.'

'What about the weapon?'

'I only saw Winifred Paull in court but she struck me as being the last person in the world to make a collection of Eskimo carvings.'

'You can't say owning one piece like that is making a collection,' Sykes pointed out.

'It was the only one in the flat then?'

'Yes, it was.'

'Well, what I said still stands. It was the last kind of thing I'd expect her to have about the place. Tell me, Sykes, you've been over the flat. Chocolate-box art . . . aren't I right about that?'

'Yes, I suppose you are. What are you suggesting, Mr Maitland? That the murderer, one of these three men whose names are on this list, brought the weapon with him?'

'Yes, I'm suggesting exactly that — to make it seem as if the murder was done on impulse, by a man whom Winifred Paull had taken up with after Ryder's arrest, for instance. And I don't think you could put forward the same theory about Caroline Ryder, not with any hope of being believed, that is. If she did the killing it was a spur of the moment affair. She snatched something that was handy . . . that's your case, isn't it?'

'Yes, it is.' Suddenly Sykes was on his feet. 'I must thank you for your hospitality, Sir Nicholas,' he went on. 'I'll try and comply with Mr Maitland's wishes. Tactfully,' he said, and exchanged a sedate smile with the older man.

Antony went to see him out, as it was then past Gibbs's immutable retiring hour. 'I'll be in touch,' Sykes told him.

'My case is adjourned until Monday,' said Antony, as though the matter were of no consequence.

'I'll try to be in touch before then.' He was at the bottom of the steps by the time he had finished speaking, said good-night more briefly than was usual with him, and made off without further ado towards Avery Street, where a taxi might still sometimes be found outside the George Hotel.

Sir Nicholas was on his feet when Antony went back to the study. 'You've done all you can,' he said. 'More than I expected. If you take my advice you'll forget all about it now and go to bed.'

Antony crossed the room to join him on the hearth-rug. 'I am tired,' he admitted. 'Is it so very obvious?' he added rather bitterly. And then, more frankly than he generally spoke even to his family, 'I can't remember a day I enjoyed less.'

Five minutes later he was back upstairs and Vera had rejoined her husband. 'Blaming himself for the murder,' she said. 'Stupid thing to do.'

'My dear,' — Sir Nicholas took the chair opposite her — 'surely you must have realised by this time that if it is possible for Antony to blame himself for some unpleasant happening he will do so, however little justification there may be.'

'I realise that, of course. But do you think that's why he's insisting they're both innocent?'

'No, I'm quite sure he's got some idea in his head about that, but whether he's right or wrong only time will tell. Sykes was helpful, and thank heavens he's discreet. There's no reason why Briggs should ever know he's doing Antony's work for him.'

'Just as well,' said Vera and sighed. 'It would be nice', she added, 'to think that the girl wasn't guilty, or the baby's father either. I mean, what a legacy for a child.'

Sir Nicholas smiled at that. He for one had never been mistaken about the fact that his wife's rather brusque attitude concealed the kindest of hearts.

Upstairs, Antony was giving Jenny an unusually disjointed account of his talk with Sykes. 'I'm grateful to him whatever happens,' he concluded, 'and I'm not at all sure that anything will come of his inquiries. Only somehow, love, the whole thing seems to have become so damned important.'

There was an obvious answer to that — 'You're doing your best' — but Jenny knew better than to make it. 'I know you've got some idea in your head,' she told him, unconsciously echoing Sir Nicholas's opinion.

'I always have ideas, love. You know better than anyone else they're very often wrong. But the thing is, Ryder said he was in my hands, and then I had to ask Mrs Ryder to trust me to get her to talk at all freely, and she said she did. That makes me feel responsible . . . and, oh lord, Jenny, what if I'm too late again?'

FRIDAY to SUNDAY, the Weekend Recess

I

It cannot be denied that the next few days were trying ones for all the members of the household at Kempenfeldt Square. Maitland, deprived of the opportunity of any direct action, could settle to nothing, though he made a good pretence of doing a day's work in chambers on Friday. As ill-luck would have it, Saturday was one of the days when Gibbs, in his perversity, insisted on serving luncheon himself. Not even Vera's beneficent influence could persuade him on this occasion that they could quite well look after themselves, which frequently they were left to do whether they liked it or not. Saturday luncheon, when the Maitlands joined Sir Nicholas and Vera for the meal, was another habit of many years' standing, but that day finding neutral subjects of conversation was a trial to all of them, and nobody was surprised when Antony got to his feet rather abruptly as soon as they had finished eating and departed without waiting for coffee, saying only over his shoulder, 'I'm going to telephone Sykes.'

He rejoined the others in the study about ten minutes later, took his time about pouring coffee for himself, and then sauntered over to the fire with a fair assumption of being at ease. 'Well?' asked Sir Nicholas sharply when the silence had continued for what seemed to him to be an unreasonably long time.

'No news,' said Antony laconically.

'Don't know how you could have expected any so soon,'

said Vera bluntly.

'It's two days,' said Maitland stubbornly.

'A day and a half,' his uncle corrected him. 'And this, may I remind you, is the weekend.'

'Poor man's entitled to some time off,' Vera put in.

'I phoned him at home and he wasn't there,' said Antony. 'Anyway, Vera, you don't expect he's doing all this trekking around himself, do you? But he must have expected my call, because he left a message for me.'

'You may as well tell us what it was,' said Sir Nicholas in a resigned tone.

'Just that the line of inquiry I suggested had been put in hand, and he'd be in touch as soon as possible. I did have a word or two with Mrs Sykes though,' he added frowning. 'She says she's hardly seen him for the last couple of days, and when he did come home it was just to sleep, and she was sure he was worried about something. I think she hoped I'd tell her what it was.'

'Did you?'

'How could I? I hoped, of course, that it means that he's taking the request I made to him the other evening seriously, but I've no means of being sure about that. It may not be anything to do with Carol Ryder's case at all.'

'I think perhaps it is,' said Sir Nicholas. 'The Chief Inspector has, I judge, a very strong sense of justice, and you appealed to that very eloquently,' he added, deliberately provoking.

'Eloquence be damned,' said Maitland. 'He'd be the last person to stand for a miscarriage of justice if he could help it. All the same . . . you see, if I don't hear something to — to make up my mind for me before Monday I don't know how to go on.' There was something very like an appeal in the last words, and for once in his life Sir Nicholas responded to it sympathetically. (Jenny said afterwards, 'Vera's influence doesn't extend only to the servants.')

'Come now,' said Sir Nicholas encouragingly, 'that's

something established. You think you know the identity of the guilty party, the man who assumed John Ryder's identity for his own purposes and later killed Winifred Paull to prevent her from giving him away.'

'I think I know, Uncle Nick. That's the trouble, I'm not sure.'

'And even if you were sure, what could you do? I understand that Winifred Paull's evidence completed the prosecution's case.'

'I still have the option of recalling Dr Gollnow.'

'Yes, I remember you telling me that. I'm not sure however, Antony, how you propose to turn that to account.'

'That's just it, I don't know either.'

'One thing I'd like you to tell us,' said Vera. 'What made you decide that Winifred Paull was lying? It can't have been her death, which you cited several times as a reason for believing in your client's innocence, because even while you were cross-examining her you'd quite obviously made up your mind.'

'That's awfully difficult to answer.' But the effort to think constructively about it could do nothing but good, as all his hearers realised. 'It's a lot of little things, Vera. While she was telling her story under Halloran's guidance she took every opportunity of pulling out the pathetic stop, and somehow her distress didn't ring at all true. Not to me, at any rate. Then — this happened during cross-examination too — she'd add things to answers quite gratuitously . . . things calculated to influence everyone against John Ryder whom she professed to love so much.'

'Natural enough,' said Vera. 'Woman scorned and all that.'

'Yes, I told myself that too.' Antony paused to smile at her. 'I don't think anybody else in the court felt as I did, and that was what worried Geoffrey and Derek so, but I told you I'd nothing to go on, only this very strong feeling that she was doing her damnedest to lead us all by the nose.'

148

'What about the inquiries Geoffrey was making into her past?' Sir Nicholas asked, for once ignoring this lapse on his nephew's part into less than elegant English.

'A dead end, so far. The flower shop she said she worked in certainly existed, but it's closed now and the owner died. Cobbold's people have talked to some friends of hers from those days. The address she gave was correct enough, but they all say she dropped them after she met the man she married — only one of them remembers that his name was Ryder — and they haven't seen anything of her since. In any case, knowing there was something wrong about her story wouldn't help us now.'

'It might form the basis for an appeal.'

'I suppose so.' Maitland didn't sound as if the idea pleased him much.

'You talked with Mrs Ryder —?'

'Worse than useless. She certainly believes in her husband . . . I didn't tell her that he'd thought for a moment that she really had killed Miss Paull. Loving wives' assertions don't go for much, and the only positive thing she could tell us would be just one more item to help damn him.'

'What was that?'

'That her arrangement with her husband was that he would ring her each evening when he was away rather than that she should ring him. And on the few occasions when she wanted to talk to him particularly and tried to get him at his sister's flat he was never there. Now that's quite natural in view of what they both told us about his habits when in London, but as I said —'

'You're quite right, I don't like it at all,' said Sir Nicholas. 'As for these feelings of yours —' He caught his wife's eye and subsided, adding rather weakly a moment or two later, 'As your aunt is about to remind me, you've been known to be right before.'

And there they left it for the time being, but — perhaps

fortunately for Antony's sanity — Chief Inspector Sykes telephoned early the following afternoon, to ask if he might come round and make his report at some convenient time.

'Come at once,' Maitland told him, explained quickly to Jenny, and rushed down to the study to banish Vera upstairs again for the time being.

'This affair is rapidly assuming all the worst elements of a French farce,' said Sir Nicholas severely when his nephew rejoined him in the study.

II

Even Sykes seemed to realise that in the short time since they had seen each other no necessity had arisen for his usual meticulous inquiries as to everyone's well-being. After greetings were exchanged, however, he did start the conversation with an apology, not too seriously intended perhaps if the note of amusement in his voice was anything to go on. 'I'm sorry that the delay has tried your patience, Mr Maitland, but I assure you your friend Inspector Mayhew and I have been very busy since we last talked together.'

Antony stared at him for a moment. 'You don't mean to say you've been doing everything yourselves,' he said in a horrified tone. 'I didn't mean that at all.'

'I think Sir Nicholas will understand my motives,' Sykes told him, 'even if you don't.'

Maitland looked at his uncle. '*Do* you understand?' he asked.

'Yes, I think so. None of us has ever been able to induce you to take seriously the fact of Chief Superintendent Briggs's animosity.'

'You mean, if it were known that Sykes is obliging me in this way . . . but I didn't think there was any chance of that. I do assure you, Chief Inspector, I've no desire to make trouble for you, nor would I have asked you to undertake work that any detective constable could have done.'

'I can trust Mayhew,' said Sykes placidly. 'And nobody could seriously take objection to our acting on information received and making a few further inquiries into Winifred Paull's murder. What was in my mind was that if it was known that you were taking a hand in the matter —'

'Meddling,' said Sir Nicholas.

'— the Chief Superintendent would be bound to put the worst construction on it.'

'Yes I know, but I still say that what he thinks doesn't matter. As long as I'm not actually indulging in any funny business —'

'If you would only choose your words with a little respect for the English language,' Sir Nicholas sighed. 'What the Chief Inspector is carefully not reminding you of is the fact that barely a month ago your movements were under surveillance by some of those very subordinates of his whom you expect him to have used in this matter. That would be bound to cause a good deal of talk among the ranks . . . am I not right, Chief Inspector?'

'You're quite right, Sir Nicholas, but we needn't argue the point,' said Sykes pacifically. 'I'd better get on with my report, or Mr Maitland will be becoming impatient again.'

'I should never have asked you to do it. I seem to have made pretty much of a fool of myself,' said Antony penitently.

'Neither Mayhew nor I would consider it time wasted if it succeeds in putting your mind at rest one way or the other,' said Sykes. 'I have to tell you to begin with that our inquiries haven't led us to suspect that there is any solution to Winifred Paull's murder except the obvious one, but perhaps the few facts we have gleaned may mean more to you than they do to us.'

'In any case I'm infinitely grateful, Chief Inspector. I say,' — he looked around him vaguely rather as though he

expected a tray to have materialised on the table by the wall
— 'wouldn't you like a drink before you start? It's a bit
early, but perhaps some tea —'

'My dear boy, you know perfectly well that's impossible,'
Sir Nicholas remonstrated. 'With Vera out . . . even if she
were allowed the run of her own kitchen which she isn't.
You see, Chief Inspector, it's customary for all of us to take
tea together on a Sunday, provided by my niece. In fact I
think you have joined us yourself on several occasions. That
being so my housekeeper will certainly be lying down, and
as for Gibbs —'

'You're as scared of him as we all are,' Antony asserted.
'Still, I agree, I don't think any tea of his providing would
be particularly pleasant, even if it didn't actually contain
any arsenic. The best thing would be if you tell us your
story, Chief Inspector, and then join us upstairs.'

'Thank you, that will be very pleasant. I'd better begin
by telling you that your idea about the photographs came to
nothing. Each one of the men you mentioned to me was
recognised vaguely by some one or other of the tenants of
the flats as having been encountered in the lift. My own
view is that that is unlikely, even if your speculations are
correct.'

'I can see it was a pretty hopeless chance, but —'

'Assuming for the moment that you are right, Mr
Maitland — without prejudice, as you might say — the man
concerned, the false John Ryder, would have visited the flat
at Brinkley Court to meet Dr Gollnow and Dennis Nesbit
during the periods that the real John Ryder was in town. He
wouldn't want to run the risk of meeting him, so I suspect
he would have used the stairs. Number 301 is only on the
second floor, after all.'

'Yes, I see your point about that. I'm sorry to have
wasted your time over it. Was there anything else?'

'This and that. I'll start with the senior man of the trio,
the only one who's unmarried, Donald Walters. He lives

152

alone, quite comfortably I think, and seems to be in easy circumstances, which isn't surprising considering his seniority. Mayhew was able to talk to some of his neighbours, under the pretext of a routine security check. Those who know the nature of his work wouldn't be surprised about that. He entertains a good deal, and has a reputation of being fond of the ladies, but of course there's absolutely no chance of providing him with an alibi for the occasions when Dr Gollnow met Mr Nesbit at Brinkley Court.'

'Naturally I didn't expect that,' Antony said a little impatiently. 'But what about the night of the murder?'

'He was at home.'

'Alone?'

'So he says.'

'That means you've talked to him,' said Antony almost accusingly.

'It seemed a good idea. In any case, it was Mayhew who saw these people, not myself.'

'But what on earth excuse could he give?'

Sykes smiled. 'I think perhaps Inspector Mayhew is an actor *manqué*,' he said. 'He flashed his own warrant card, which none of them asked to examine more closely, and represented himself as a member of the SIS. He didn't find out anything more about John Ryder's associates during his periods in London, which was the ostensible reason for his visit, but it wasn't really difficult to bring up the subject of the trial, and consequently of Winifred Paull's murder.'

'But he couldn't actually ask them —'

'No, of course not. We'll come to the others in a moment, but Mr Walters remarked on his sympathy for the girl, whom he had seen giving evidence. He said that one would have thought she'd been hurt enough, and then he seemed to recollect himself and expressed some sympathy for Mrs Ryder as well. And then he added something like, ''I was sitting here reading a mystery story as it happened, which seemed ironical when I heard next day what had happened".'

'I wonder if Mayhew got any impression whether the three men were friends with each other outside the office.'

'Braithwaite and Gibbon, yes. They're contemporaries and seem to be good friends. I heard the same thing from all three of them, that there was some exchange of hospitality with their superior officer, but more or less of a formal nature.'

'What impression did Mayhew get of Donald Walters, as a person I mean?'

'A favourable one, as he did of the others except perhaps in the case of William Gibbon. He was talking to him and Mrs Gibbon at the same time, and he thought the man's attitude was rather spiteful towards his former colleague. So was Mrs Gibbon's for that matter; she said she thought he was wasting his time inquiring about John's friends, obviously he'd been completely taken up with that woman he'd married bigamously. And I must say, Mr Maitland, we encountered a small puzzle here.'

'What was that?' asked Antony eagerly.

'Nothing very significant, except that Mayhew got the impression that the Gibbons lived rather better than the Braithwaites did. That doesn't seem altogether consistent, considering that Ernest Braithwaite is a little the elder, and has been in that particular job several years longer.'

'I see.' Maitland looked unaccountably downcast at the information.

'I'm afraid it's not much help to us. I was sufficiently interested to put a few inquiries in motion into their circumstances, and it seems that William Gibbon came into a quite considerable legacy some years back.'

'That wouldn't explain his malicious attitude towards John Ryder, or Edith Gibbon's attitude either,' said Antony, frowning.

'I'm afraid I can't explain it, but one further fact may be

154

of interest to you. An aunt of Mr Gibbon's, a talkative lady with no inhibitions, whom I visited myself, told me about the money, and then clapped her hand over her mouth as though she'd been indiscreet. Then she said she had to be careful who she told about this because Edith didn't know. William had a very secretive nature, and besides was of the opinion that all women were spendthrifts.'

For some reason Antony's spirits seemed to revive immediately. 'Alibis,' he said.

'I'm afraid I can't be of help to you there either. There was a film Ernest Braithwaite wanted to see, something his wife didn't care for, so they got a snack when they left the court and she went home alone. As he was going to the first house, we checked up on that, he'd have had plenty of time to go to Brinkley Court and be away again by the time Mrs Ryder arrived. As for the other two, the Gibbons, Mayhew said he didn't even have to manoeuvre the conversation, except so far as the trial. Mrs Gibbon said immediately what an ordeal it was giving evidence, and she knew her husband felt the same way. Not to mention the shock when Winifred Paull collapsed. She said they both went home and were good for nothing for the rest of the evening. Mayhew thought, but this was only an impression, Mr Maitland —'

'I think I can perhaps guess what you're going to say, Chief Inspector. Mayhew thought that William Gibbon looked a little surprised when she said that.'

'Yes, but as I said —'

'Don't worry, I won't give the remark any more weight than you feel I should.' There was still an unaccountable air of complacency about Antony, and his uncle gave him a look in which suspicion and worry were nicely blended. 'Well, as to the other matter, the question of one of them being the false John Ryder, I take it there was nothing more to be gleaned than there was about Mr Walters.'

'I suppose from the fact that we've learned that Ernest and Jane Braithwaite's tastes don't always coincide we may assume that he would have had the opportunity of going to Brinkley Court if he wished without her knowledge. As to the Gibbons —'

'I'll make another guess, Chief Inspector. That Mrs Gibbon took the opportunity of telling Mayhew, unasked, that she and her husband always did everything together.'

'I'm beginning to think, Mr Maitland, that you know more about this matter than you've told me,' said Sykes rather severely.

'Know is a rather large word, but I have my suspicions.'

'Then don't you think it's time you stopped fencing with me and came out into the open with them.'

'Yes, I will in a moment. You haven't told me yet whether you learned anything about the ostensible reason for Mayhew's visit to these three men.'

'Not a thing. Do you mean to tell me', said Sykes, for once startled out of his placidity, 'that for all this smooth talk you've been giving me you still aren't sure yourself of your client's innocence?'

'I'm as sure as one can be of anything in this uncertain world. Would I try to deceive you, Chief Inspector?' he added lightly.

'I'm bound to say, Mr Maitland, I think you would if it suited your ends. However, I'll take what you say as true. None of them knew anything of John Ryder beyond seeing him in the office and their occasional social contacts when he was in town. He talked of his home in Wolverhampton, and hadn't much to say about the time he spent here, which could be construed in either of two ways. He was secretive because he was living a double life, or his life with Mrs Caroline Ryder was the only thing that mattered to him.'

'I suppose I should thank you for that concession to my point of view,' said Antony meekly. 'There's just one other thing which I didn't anticipate being able to ask you. Since Mayhew has actually been inside each of their homes —'

'You're wondering where the Eskimo carving might have

156

come from, if it wasn't already in Winifred Paull's flat.'

'Yes, precisely. It could have been part of a collection, and I have it on Ryder's authority that there's nothing of that kind on view in any of their homes. Not in the rooms he's seen at least. But I thought Mayhew might have been a little more observant about the *kind* of decoration each of them favours.'

'He thought Mr Walter's flat was rather lifeless,' said Sykes promptly. 'He only saw the living-room, of course, and said it had no more personal touches about it than an hotel room would have. There were one or two pictures, but Mayhew said they were modern stuff, he didn't understand them.'

'I thought you said he lived rather comfortably.'

'Yes, but comfort and taste don't always go together. Everything looked expensive, and when Mayhew was offered a drink — which he accepted, being in no sense on duty — there were several very fancy cut-glass decanters, and there was nothing wrong with the Scotch he offered either. As for the Braithwaites, their taste ran to chintz and dark oak, which Mayhew said rather austerely would have been more suitable in a country cottage.'

'That will be of Jane Braithwaite's choosing,' said Antony, nodding.

'Very likely. Mayhew liked the Gibbons' set-up best, modern and comfortable and expensive as I told you. I don't see that there's anything there to help you.'

'The Eskimo carving would have been quite out of place along with the Braithwaites' chintzes,' said Antony thoughtfully. 'If it belonged to Walters it looks as if it must have been somewhere else in the flat. While as for the Gibbons —'

'Anything might fit in with the modern setting Mayhew described,' said Sykes. 'He's the one you favour, isn't he?'

For a moment Antony succumbed to the temptation to allow the silence to lengthen. 'Oh no, Chief Inspector,' he

157

said then, '*I* think our man's Donald Walters.'

III

Sykes's reply didn't come quickly either. Sir Nicholas, after looking from one to the other of them rather quizzically for a moment said trenchantly, 'Come now, Antony, you've had your fun. You mustn't pull the Chief Inspector's leg any longer, as my dear wife would say.'

This remark had the effect of making Antony lose the thread of the conversation for a moment. Sir Nicholas had always looked with indulgence on Vera's occasional lapses into colloquialisms which he would have condemned roundly in anyone else, but the fact that he occasionally emulated her was still sufficient to deprive his nephew of speech. 'Very well, I'll tell you,' he said finally. 'The trouble is I don't think either of you will find my explanations at all convincing.'

'I'll be glad to hear what you have to say, of course,' said Sykes, breaking his silence, 'but I'm bound to tell you that if we accept your hypothesis any indications there are seem to point to William Gibbon. You took the point that his wife was over-ready with an alibi for him on the night of the murder —'

'Yes, and there were other things. I don't mind telling you he had me worried, but now I think I can see why. Unless . . . was this legacy you spoke of genuine, not payment for some dirty work or other?'

'No, quite genuine. But that doesn't preclude the fact that there may have been other payments as well.'

'You see, what stuck in my gullet was Edith Gibbon's story in court. She said she saw John Ryder with Winifred Paull once, and had later identified her. If she was lying it was a carefully prepared lie; she'd taken the trouble to find out what Miss Paull looked like. I think I know how she did that. Miss Paull mentioned being pestered by telephone calls, and even by one woman who made an excuse to visit her flat, but why should Mrs Gibbon have bothered? Naturally, it looked as if she was trying to protect her husband, but now that's all explained.'

'It may be to you, Mr Maitland,' said Sykes grimly, 'but it isn't to me.'

'He never told her about the money he'd inherited,' said Antony patiently. 'I'd say she's quite intelligent enough to have wondered about that, and when all this business came up there must have been some doubt in her mind as to whether her husband might be involved in some way. So, as I say, she was trying to protect him, but in my opinion without any reason.'

'And you've absolved the Braithwaites too?'

'Oh yes, I think so. Just think about Donald Walters' evidence for a moment.'

'I wasn't there,' said Sykes.

'No, of course you weren't, but you can take my word for it, can't you? He did his own share of trying to damn John Ryder, he did it with suitable reluctance but there was no doubting his intent. When he denied knowing Dr Gollnow he was just a little too emphatic about it, and he talked about Ryder having spoken of "the little woman", which I'll take my oath is a phrase he'd never have used. Furthermore — and don't either of you dare say that this isn't a good point — he started some of his sentences with the phrase "to be frank with you". That's generally the prelude to a lie.'

'Good heavens, boy,' Sir Nicholas was moved to protest, 'you can't base a case on somebody's way of expressing himself.'

'I said it wouldn't convince you, but I also say that all these little things added together mean something. There are two further points, nothing to do with Walters' evidence. The first is something that Ryder told me, and it's

159

the thing that set me thinking about Walters in the first place. He said Walters had been with Wycherley's since he was an apprentice, and he thought he was unlucky not to have risen further in the firm than he had because he's an exceptionally bright chap. One of his subordinates, I think it was Braithwaite, had said to Ryder that Mr Walters was very strong on ideas (I think that was his phrase) but not so good at applying them. Ryder also told me that the present managing director of the firm had been an apprentice at the same time. That could have bred some resentment, and resentment . . . well, that can lead almost anywhere.'

Neither of his listeners made any immediate comment, but after a moment Sykes said, 'And your second point, Mr Maitland?'

'That if the murderer brought his weapon with him it must have been the only one of the three men who was unmarried. If the thing had been in either of their homes, don't you think Jane Braithwaite or Edith Gibbon would have noticed that it was missing? Edith certainly was quite willing to lie to protect her husband, but do you think he'd have risked it?'

'That's a good point,' said Sykes consideringly. 'But it still presupposes your John Ryder's innocence.'

'Of which I, for one, am convinced.'

'What are you going to do?' inquired Sir Nicholas, with an apprehension that was normally quite foreign to his nature.

'Nothing that will involve either of my accomplices,' said Antony, with a sudden, brilliant smile in the detective's direction. 'I'm far too grateful to you and Mayhew for that. My only doubt was the point I've mentioned about Gibbon, and you've set my mind at rest about that.'

'Even so,' said Sykes bluntly, 'I don't see what you can do now. Donald Walters has already given evidence —'

'But, as I reminded my uncle the other day, I still have the option of recalling Dr Gollnow. And that's exactly what

160

I'm going to do.'

'If you think you can get him to retract his identification —'

'I don't know till I try, do I? No,' he added despondently, and all the weariness was back in his voice again, 'I'm not particularly optimistic and heaven knows what Geoffrey and Derek will say. But when there's only one way open to you you've got to take it. We haven't a defence worth a damn.'

'I should have said', Sir Nicholas remarked, very coldly, 'that you've already done enough to alienate the court. And if the man is innocent — this Donald Walters, I mean — you may do him irreparable harm, both personally and in his career.'

'Do you think I haven't thought of that? I'll be careful, Uncle Nick, and the worst that can happen is that Halloran will have the laugh of me, and I'll make a fool of myself. That's not what I'm afraid of.'

'What then?' asked his uncle more gently.

'I'm afraid of a man and a woman being convicted of crimes they didn't commit, and if you must have the full story,' he added rather savagely, 'I'm afraid of the child being born in prison and growing up to find out later what his parents are supposed to have done.' He broke off there, gave a laugh in which there was no amusement at all, and heaved himself out of his chair. 'I hope I've said enough to make you realise how grateful I am to you, Chief Inspector,' he said formally. 'And now for the lord's sake, let's forget about it for a moment and go upstairs and have some tea.'

It wasn't until an hour later when Sykes had left them and Jenny and Vera had disappeared kitchenwards with the tea things that Sir Nicholas said to his nephew, 'You were good enough to be honest with me about your worries, Antony, but I have an idea there's something you've left out.'

'Everything I said was true,' said Maitland defensively.

'I'm sure it was. All the same I have the strangest feeling —'

161

'You're right, of course,' said Antony, capitulating. 'It's Dr Gollnow.'

'You told me once you rather liked him,' said Sir Nicholas, casting his mind back.

'Yes, I do. And nobody knows yet whether he's sincere in his desire to seek asylum or not. If he is and nobody believes him —'

'You can't take responsibility for the whole world's troubles, Antony,' Sir Nicholas told him. 'Just at the moment, if I were you, I'd concentrate on what you're going to say to the good doctor tomorrow when you meet him in court.'

MONDAY, *The Fourth Day of the Trial*

Geoffrey protested less than he had expected when he announced his intention of recalling Dr Gollnow, and a weekend's reflection had obviously convinced Derek too that it would be futile to reason any further with his leader. John Ryder was looking more strained, Antony thought, than at any time since the trial began; Geoffrey's visit, which had been intended to reassure him as to his wife's well-being, had obviously not been altogether successful. And after all, what could the solicitor have said? That Caroline was as well as could be expected?

Waiting for the judge, Maitland took the opportunity to observe that although his younger colleagues seemed to have been excused further attendance, Donald Walters was still among those present. This was more than he had dared to hope, but no doubt Head Office had instructed him to see the matter through to the end, so as to be able to report on anything that concerned them.

When the time came, Antony made his request confidently. 'Your lordship will recall that it was agreed —'

'I remember my promise, Mr Maitland, that Dr Gollnow might be recalled if you so desired,' said Carruthers, not allowing him to finish. 'The witness has been escorted back to court this morning, and can be easily produced if that is your wish.'

'I do indeed desire it, my lord. In the absence of Miss Paull's further testimony —'

This time it was Halloran who interrupted. 'Winifred Paull had concluded her testimony,' he said. 'I had no

163

further questions for her.'

'My learned friend will forgive my somewhat careless way of putting it. I should have said, in the absence of an opportunity for me to cross-examine her at greater length —' This time he did not even attempt to finish the sentence. Mr Justice Carruthers eyed him for a long moment, and the gleam in his lordship's eye was almost certainly one of amusement. 'Very well, Mr Maitland, very well,' he agreed, and Antony could almost have sworn that he added under his breath, 'What kind of a surprise do you have for us today?'

So Dr Boris Gollnow was called again and brought into the court, his escorts, as the judge had called them, in close attendance. Antony's heart sank a little when he saw that the Russian's look of confidence was in no way abated. The judge waited until he was settled comfortably in the witness box, and then greeted him courteously, reminding him of the continuing efficacy of his oath.

'Ah, that oath!' said Dr Gollnow, shaking his head as though at his own folly. 'My lord, I must admit to you that after so many years of professing atheism — which is a condition of membership in the party you understand — I was in some doubt as to whether taking the oath might call down on my head some fearful retribution from an angry deity.'

'Dr Gollnow!' Mr Justice Carruthers was eyeing him askance. 'You assured the court before you gave your evidence that you believed in God, and that you would prefer to swear on a Christian Bible, rather than merely to affirm your evidence.'

'Certainly, my lord. I am only saying that practice does not always follow belief, but for the rest I am indulging in a little pleasantry, to hide my nervousness.'

'Very well, doctor. You may proceed, Mr Maitland.' Carruthers leaned back and picked up his pen as Antony turned to the witness. And if you were half as nervous as I am, counsel thought, eyeing the Russian a trifle resentfully, perhaps we'd have some chance of getting somewhere.

'Are you familiar with the saying, Dr Gollnow,' he asked without preamble, 'that three may keep a secret, if two of them are dead?'

Just for a moment he thought he surprised a look of anxiety in the witness's eyes. 'I have heard it,' said Gollnow slowly. 'Your Benjamin Franklin, I believe. Or no,' he corrected himself, 'he was not an Englishman, but what I have heard called a Damn Yankee. Am I right?'

'That would depend on what time of his life you were talking about,' said Maitland seriously. 'But I don't wish to discuss history. It's what he said I want you to think about.'

'So I gather, and I know you'll forgive me for saying, Mr Maitland, that I do not understand its relevance.'

'I'm not quite sure, doctor, in your present circumstances, how much you know about what's going on in the world.'

'I've been very kindly treated, I assure you. I have books, of course, and a number of newspapers each day.'

'Then you know, I presume, that Winifred Paull, whom you knew as Mrs John Ryder, is dead?'

'Yes, I have read of it.' He shifted a little, settling himself more comfortably as though for a long chat. 'To tell you the truth I should have been glad enough to talk of it to one of my guards, but they felt that anything at all to do with this case —'

'And very properly,' Maitland agreed. 'And I have been guilty of using a euphemism, Dr Gollnow. I said "her death", when I should have said "her murder".'

'It is very sad, of course, but in either event I don't see how it affects me.'

'You are now the only living witness to John Ryder's identity.'

'But surely that is not any longer in dispute.'

'I'm sorry if I confused you. I meant to the fact that my

165

client, John Ryder, is the man who introduced you to Dennis Nesbit, and in whose flat the exchanges of information took place.'

'I still do not understand you.'

'Think of that fact for a moment, and think also of the quotation I mentioned to you just now.'

'If you mean that I too should fear for my life . . . oh, no, Mr Maitland, I have no worries on that score. My friends here, and their associates, take very good care of me.'

'But you think that without this care there might be cause to fear?'

'I did not say so.' Again there was that slight sense that the witness had withdrawn into himself a little.

'If you did not say so in so many words, at least you implied it.'

'My knowledge of your language —'

'Is, I believe, as good as my own.'

'You must surely realise that in my present position my own countrymen —'

'Yes, I've no doubt that they'd like to lay hands on you,' counsel agreed. 'But we were talking about Winifred Paull's death.'

'My lord!' Halloran was on his feet. 'I can appreciate my friend's need to clutch at straws in this matter, but surely this line of questioning is taking us nowhere. Miss Paull's death seems to be only indirectly concerned with this case.'

'What have you to say to that, Mr Maitland?'

There was need to be careful here. Mr Justice Carruthers would give the defence whatever latitude his sense of fairness dictated, but there was a definite line beyond which he couldn't be pushed. 'I do not think, my lord, that it would be right for us in this court to take any cognisance of the police theory as to who killed Winifred Paull.'

'You're quite right, Mr Maitland, nothing could be more improper. But I think Mr Halloran is concerned besides with the relevance of the questions you're asking.'

'If your lordship will give me leave I think I can demonstrate their relevance.'

'Very well, Mr Maitland, but I think I should remind you that I shall not countenance any overstepping of the line of what is reasonable. If you are trying to scare the witness —'

'Certainly not, my lord!' said Antony, shocked.

'I was about to add that I don't think you'll succeed, and I don't think it would do you any good if you did. However, bearing that in mind, you may proceed with your cross-examination.'

'I'm obliged to your lordship. Dr Gollnow, how long is it since you went to see Sir Charles Daniell?'

'It was the tenth of February. About five weeks ago.'

'And what exactly was your intention in so doing?'

'I do not like the word defect, but that was what I wished to do. To have nothing more to do with communism, with its suppression of all individuality. To live as a free man among free men.'

'And is that what you've been doing, doctor, during this last five weeks?'

'Far from it. I have been —'

Maitland held up a hand quickly to stop him. 'We don't want to know where you have been living, doctor. But his lordship has spoken of your escorts, whom you called your guards. Was this freedom?'

'It was no more than I expected. There would be questions, there would be doubts as to the truthfulness of what I had to tell. There has been delay because of this trial. But in the end I hope there will be a new identity, a new life.'

'Let us speak for a moment of the term ''guards'',' said Maitland. 'And in that we include the people who have been asking you questions. When did it occur to you, Dr Gollnow, that there was some doubt about the truth of your statements?'

'I had expected there would be doubts at first.'

'But haven't they persisted rather longer than you expected? I put it to you, Dr Gollnow, and I should like you to think very carefully before answering, when you heard that Winifred Paull had identified my client as the man she had married, the man who acted as go-between in your dealings with Dennis Nesbit, were you not a little afraid that if you contradicted her, it was you who would be thought the liar?'

'Mr Maitland has laid no foundation for these insinuations against the witness, my lord,' said Halloran angrily. 'He has no grounds —'

'I have every reason and right to put these questions,' said Antony hotly. Then, recollecting himself and turning to the judge, 'I submit, my lord, that Winifred Paull's death makes every difference. It is our case that she was killed to prevent her from identifying the man she married, or went through a form of marriage with.'

'She had already identified the prisoner in the dock,' said Halloran flatly.

'To prevent her from changing her testimony,' Antony insisted.

Mr Justice Carruthers looked from one to the other of them. 'And you think Dr Gollnow may be in danger of the same fate?' he asked.

'No my lord, because of the fact that he is still under strict surveillance. When the day comes for that to cease Dr Boris Gollnow will cease to exist also. I don't know what his new identity will be, I hope for his sake something quite unrecognisable, but —'

'Then how does all this help you?'

'My lord, I want to make him see the futility of his action. Winifred Paull lied in identifying my client, because she wished to protect the man who had assumed his identity. Dr Gollnow can have no such reason, and if it can be proved that he has lied and is persisting in his lie, don't you think that will make the people who have responsibility for granting him asylum or not even more sceptical than they are already?'

'Yes, Mr Maitland, I see your point, but it is all predicated on your client's innocence, isn't it?'

'Indeed it is, my lord.'

'And if Dr Gollnow is telling the truth, has been telling the truth all along, what then?'

'It can surely do no harm, my lord, to let me pursue the matter a little further. Do you remember the careful wording of the witness's identification, here in this court. "I recognise that man." Certainly he did, as someone he had seen before in the presence, I presume, of Mr K. and Mr Y.; what he did *not* say was that he had known him before that confrontation.'

'What do you think, Mr Halloran?' Carruthers asked Counsel for the Prosecution, who was still on his feet.

'I think, my lord, that as a firm identification had already been made by the woman Ryder was living with, it was perfectly natural — '

'I agree with you, Mr Halloran, but that is not the point.' For once the judge sounded a little testy. 'Shall I allow Mr Maitland to proceed on the lines he seems to have mapped out for himself?'

Bruce Halloran regarded his opponent for a long moment. 'I have no further objection,' he said surprisingly, and threw himself down in his seat again, leaving Antony wondering whether he had made an unexpected convert, or whether he was being invited to make a fool of himself.

'Very well, Mr Maitland,' — the judge's voice interrupted his thoughts — 'you may proceed.'

'I'm obliged to your lordship.' Obliged to you too, Halloran, even if you do think I haven't a chance of proving what I say. 'Very well, Dr Gollnow, let us go back to the John Ryder you knew.'

All this time the witness had been listening with an air of

polite bewilderment. 'Is it permitted that I ask you a question?' he inquired.

'It's rather irregular, but —' Maitland glanced at the judge.

'The whole proceedings have become so irregular,' said Carruthers, 'as under your guidance they're apt to do, Mr Maitland, that I see no harm in the witness's request.'

'It's a very small matter that I wish to ask this gentleman. Has anyone suggested that this Winifred Paull you speak of, whom I must still think of as Mrs Ryder, was lying when she made the identification?'

'The prisoner has denied that he knew her at all, let alone had lived with her as her husband.'

'You'll forgive me for saying that in the circumstances I should expect nothing else.'

'Perhaps not, but I too am convinved that she was lying. With my colleagues, of course,' he added, less than honestly.

'I had suspected as much. Very well, Mr Maitland,' said the witness, with an air of condescension for which Antony could be cheerfully have hit him, 'proceed with your questions.'

'We were going to talk about the John Ryder you knew.'

'You see him before you.'

'Certainly I do.' Maitland leaned forward, giving every word its full weight. 'He is certainly in this courtroom and has been since he gave evidence for the prosecution, but I suggest to you that your friend, whom I've no doubt you knew as John Ryder, is not the man in the dock.'

'And you tell me that you have your reasons for saying that?'

'Dr Gollnow, may I remind you that for the moment it is I who am asking the questions? I *have* a good many reasons, all of them good ones, but we'll come to them in a moment. Just now I want you to tell me about John Ryder as you knew him. You told my friend, as I remember, that he

170

introduced himself to you one evening, and offered to put you in touch with Dennis Nesbit, who was prepared to sell information to your government.'

'Yes, that is correct. But there was a little more — do you say, fencing? — between us before anything so definite was said.'

'That we understand. It was further agreed that he himself would make premises available for your meeting, and supply the equipment necessary when there were documents to be copied and so on?'

'That is also correct.'

'We're not concerned with any payments that may have been made to Mr Nesbit, but I presume that Mr Ryder also received some consideration for his help.'

'Payments were made to cover the purchase of the necessary equipment, and the rental of the flat. In addition . . . speaking from memory I cannot give you exact figures and my books — such as they were — have been impounded by your own authorities, but I can tell you that the payments were not ungenerous.'

'Would it surprise you to know that as far as has been discovered, all such payments, including the ones for the rental, were banked in the name of Winifred Ryder — Winifred Paull, who called herself Mrs John Ryder — and that her so-called husband had no part in these transactions?'

'Perhaps that is a custom in this country.'

'Not, I think, to that extent. There is also no trace that any of this money found its way to my client's home in Wolverhampton.'

'No doubt he found himself in an awkward situation, having two wives.'

'That is a matter, Dr Gollnow, upon which the jury have still to pronounce.' (Maitland, in spite of his concentration on the witness or perhaps for the very reason that it was for the moment so intense, found a tune from *Trial By Jury*

171

echoing persistently in his head: *In the reign of James the Second it was generally reckoned as a rather serious crime to have two wives at a time.*) 'What was *your* impression of the relationship between the man you knew as John Ryder, and the woman you knew as his wife? Who may actually be his wife, for all I know.'

'I don't think I had any particular impression about that.'

'Were they rapturously in love? Jogging along comfortably together? At each other's throats?'

'You give me a wide choice, Mr Maitland. If I must choose one of your three descriptions it would certainly be the middle one.'

'Can you enlarge on that?'

The witness hesitated. 'I saw no open signs of affection,' he said, when the silence had grown long enough to become uneasy. 'But no signs of dissension either.'

'In other words, they might have easily been a couple engaged together in some business enterprise as man and wife.'

'You forget, that was all I knew or thought I knew of their relationship . . . that they were married.'

'Looking back on it now —'

'I don't think I know the answer to your question.'

'But it was your impression that your John Ryder lived in the flat, 301, Brinkley Court, during the time he was in London?'

'I had no reason to think differently.'

'You knew his circumstances?'

'I knew about his work in Wolverhampton, but not about his wife there.'

'In other words, he went to some trouble to give you details of his situation.'

'You forget, Mr Maitland, the nature of our business together was such as to demand complete trust between us. It was necessary that I knew something of his circumstances.'

172

Touché, thought Maitland, and saw Derek's hand pause for a second and then go on smoothly with what he was writing. 'Didn't it occur to you, when first he told you of the rather tiresome way in which his job was arranged, that he was a little old not to have obtained a more secure position in his company?'

'Yes, but —' Again he broke off and turned rather deliberately to look at the prisoner. 'I made no inquiries as to his age, Mr Maitland, but I should think him no more than in his early thirties. not many men are completely established at that age.'

'That's true, and it's a perfectly reasonable remark as regards to my client, the *real* John Ryder. I suggest to you, however, that the man you met resembled him hardly at all.'

'You are mistaken.'

'Am I, Dr Gollnow? I also suggest that your first impulse just now was to agree with me that the John Ryder you met was rather older than you would have expected from his job description.'

'You are mistaken,' said the witness again.

'We shall see. Now, doctor, may we go back to what you told us about your first meeting with John Ryder. You said, and you will correct me if I quote you wrongly, that you had seen too many men in the grip of an ideal willing to treat communism as a religion.'

'That is what I said as far as I remember it. But I made one small qualification, Mr Maitland, which you have omitted. I said, especially young men.'

'So you did.' There was no sign in Antony's tone that that was exactly the answer he had wanted. 'A man might betray his country for an ideal —'

'I understand that very well,' said Dr Gollnow rather sadly. 'It is, as you realise, what I myself am doing.'

'So you tell us. Out of an ideal,' Maitland repeated. 'You've been in this business a long time, Dr Gollnow, have

173

you not?'

'Yes, that is true. I have given all details —'

'They do not concern us here,' said Antony hastily. 'What I wanted to ask you was whether, in the course of this long experience, you have ever come across a man — an older man possibly — who betrayed his country out of a sense of disillusionment, out of the feeling perhaps that his own qualities had never been properly recognised and rewarded?'

'That state of mind is not unfamiliar to me.'

'Then I suggest to you, Dr Gollnow, that it is precisely what you saw in the man who introduced himself as John Ryder. An older man than my client, and disillusioned, as I said.'

'You have a very vivid imagination, Mr Maitland.'

Antony smiled at him suddenly. 'Let's leave my imagination out of it,' he suggested. 'You haven't answered my question.'

'Your suggestion was false,' said the witness precisely.

'Was it, Dr Gollnow? Then let me remind you that, except for some small conjectural matters, the case that the man who acted as go-between between yourself and Dennis Nesbit was in fact my client John Ryder rests solely upon your evidence.'

'And on Mrs Ryder's sworn statement, I believe, which must have been recorded,' said the witness quickly.

'On that too. It's odd, isn't it, that I wasn't allowed the opportunity of finishing my cross-examination of her?'

'Odd perhaps, but I do not know what it is supposed to signify.'

'That she might have been brought to retract her identification; or that some man — the man you knew as John Ryder for instance — may have believed that that was possible.'

The witness didn't answer that directly. 'There was also the passport found in the flat they occupied,' he said with an air of triumph.

'I'm glad you reminded me of that, Dr Gollnow. You see, part of my reconstruction of what happened rests very largely on that passport.'

'How could that be?'

'If someone deliberately assumed the identity of my client, John Ryder, for the purpose of his dealings with you, and previously with the colleagues you mentioned, it must have been someone who knew him very well indeed and who had access to the passport.'

'That would certainly follow,' said the witness, nodding. 'But I do not think it proves your point.'

'That, doctor, is for the jury to decide.' For some time now Halloran's continued silence had been causing Maitland some disquiet. That the judge was silent too was less worrying, given what he knew of Carruthers' character, but he was nearing the end now and no nearer his objective so far as he could see. 'My client will testify in due course that the passport was kept in his briefcase, that he had not used it or had occasion to look at it for some considerable time, and that the most likely place where an opportunity existed for its removal was at the London office of his firm, where he was in the habit of leaving the case standing beside his desk.' He didn't dare look at Donald Walters as he spoke, but Derek must have sensed the query in his mind and pushed a note along the desk so that he could read it: *He's sweating*, it said succinctly.

And now Mr Justice Carruthers at last intervened. 'I'm sure these conjectures of yours are very interesting, Mr Maitland,' he said, 'but I think you will agree with me that your closing address would have been a more suitable occasion to bring them forward.'

'There is still the matter of proof, my lord.'

'I'm glad you have retained so much grasp on reality. May I ask you, Mr Maitland, are you hoping to get this proof from the witness, Dr Boris Gollnow?'

'I was hoping so, my lord.' There was a note of despair in his tone that he hadn't intended, and perhaps it was this that softened the judge's mood.

'I suppose I should be grateful that you didn't add, "If your lordship hadn't interfered" to that remark,' Carruthers said with a smile.

'I've two further questions I should like to put to Dr Gollnow, my lord,' said Antony hopefully. 'Or rather . . . well, one isn't exactly a question,' he admitted.

'No more speeches intended for the jury's ears?'

'The question is a simple matter of fact, my lord. For the rest, one — no two — points for Dr Gollnow's consideration. That is all.'

'Mr Halloran?'

'Since my learned friend has already been granted so much latitude — ' Halloran rumbled, and Maitland thought suddenly, they're both curious. But for all the good it will do me . . . this is a tough old bird, as I might have known, and quite capable of parrying an attack from any angle. But then he remembered his first impression of the man, a man brought up under a creed that cared nothing for the rights of the individual, but who nevertheless to Antony's eyes seemed to have retained some measure at least of humanity. If there was any hope now . . .

'You may proceed, Mr Maitland,' Carruthers was saying rather impatiently, from which Antony gathered it wasn't the first time he had been so addressed. He bowed to the bench, which he hoped was sufficient apology, and turned again to face the witness, though still pausing for a moment before he spoke.

'You have said you see the newspapers, doctor. Did the one you read this morning mention the weapon with which Winifred Paull was killed?'

'An Eskimo carving of some kind.'

'Are you familiar with such things?'

'I've seen them here in the shops.'

'Then can you tell me — you say you visited the flat at Brinkley court many times — whether you ever saw anything of the nature there? I'm sure the witness Mr K. will be pleased to answer that question,' he added when the witness did not reply immediately, 'but I don't wish to put the court to the trouble of recalling him unless it is necessary.'

'You said one question, Mr Maitland,' the judge reminded him.

'May I submit, my lord, that they were all part of the same one?'

'Perhaps, but Winifred Paull's death is nothing to do with the present case.'

'My lord — forgive me — she was a witness for the prosecution, one of their chief witnesses. I don't think that either of us can say at this juncture whether her death is relevant to this matter or not.'

'Very well, the witness may answer.'

Perhaps the judge's intervention had been a good thing, in giving Boris Gollnow time to think. 'If it is of any help to you, Mr Maitland,' he said — and quite obviously he felt there was no chance of that — 'I have never seen such a thing in the Ryder's flat. Nor do I think it would have been to Mrs Ryder's taste,' he added thoughtfully.

'If you have seen such items in the shop windows, you must have noticed that they are expensive. I don't think there was anybody who'd have purchased it solely for use as a weapon, but if it was already in his possession — '

'But surely something simpler and less expensive could have been found.'

'The idea was, I think,' — just for the moment there might have been no more than two of them in the courtroom — 'that it should look as if the murder had been committed by someone who snatched up a weapon already to hand. I have been looking over my own household, which I'm sure is typical of many others, and except for the fire irons — I

177

understand there are no fireplaces in Brinkley Court — and a few odd tools in a drawer in the kitchen there's nothing that would fill the bill. But the police are thorough and it's only a matter of time before they discover where the carving came from, either by finding someone who saw it in the owner's home, or by tracing the shop where it was purchased.'

'I understood that the case was closed.'

'No murder case is ever closed until the jury has delived its verdict,' said Maitland sententiously. 'And even then, if new evidence comes to hand . . . have you thought of that, Dr Gollnow?'

'Naturally not, but I bow to your superior knowledge of these matters,' said the witness ironically.

And that, thought Antony despairingly, is as far as we're going to get. 'Dr Gollnow,' he said, 'I won't mince matters with you. I believe that your identification of my client as the John Ryder you knew was a complete fabrication, occasioned by your fear that if you contradicted Winifred Paull in this matter it was you who would be believed to be lying. The corollary to that would be, you believed, that you would be denied the political asylum you so much wish for.' He paused, but the witness made no attempt to speak. 'Have you given any thought to the consequences of your action to anyone but yourself? To the two young people, John and Caroline Ryder, who have been swept up willy-nilly into this affair; and to the future of the child — their child — who will be born in prison in four months' time, and who will live out his life under the shadow of these events. Can you live out the rest of *your* life, in freedom as you told us so affectingly, in the knowledge that their freedom is being denied them solely through your lack of candour. And, let's make no mistake about it, I know the truth now — I make no apology for that assertion, my lord — and sooner or later everyone will know it. I don't know how that can be managed, but I shall manage it. Don't you

178

care at all?'

There was a long moment of stunned silence. Geoffey said afterwards it was as though the court were holding its collective breath. Then the witness stirred, and gave the man who was questioning him a smile in which there was no more than a tinge of regret. 'It isn't proof, Mr Maitland,' he said.

'I'm very well aware of the fact.'

'Nor do I think, for all your fine words, that it will be very easy to find that proof. All the same, I think I will tell you. Since you know so much,' he added, and turned to face the judge directly. 'Mr Maitland was quite right about my motives, my lord,' he said, 'and quite right too about the fact that I lied. I did know the man who put me into contact with Mr Nesbit as John Ryder, and everything I told the men who interrogated me about him was what he had told me himself. But I never saw the prisoner in the dock in my life until I was asked to identify him.'

Stillness became pandemonium. The usher bellowed for silence, there were threats to clear the court, and when some semblance of order had been restored Mr Justice Carruthers said in his quiet way, and quite unnecessarily one might have thought, 'That is a complete reversal of your previous evidence, Dr Gollnow.'

'It is, my lord.'

'Then I think that there is one further question you must answer, which I am sure Mr Maitland is only waiting for the opportunity to put to you. What can you tell us about this other man, the man who assumed the identity of the John Ryder who stands accused in this court?'

'I can do better than that, my lord. Mr Maitland mentioned earlier his belief that the person concerned had given evidence, and was at present in the court. Also that John Ryder's passport could easily have been stolen at the office he used in London. My lord, you will recall that I have been present here only when giving my evidence; I can identify the man, but I couldn't have invented the identification from the information at my disposal.'

'He's actually in the court?' asked Mr Justice Carruthers incredulously. 'I thought Mr Maitland was merely indulging in his well-known sense of the dramatic.'

'No, my lord, not in this case.'

'Then perhaps, Dr Gollnow, you will point him out to us.'

'Certainly my lord. I still don't know his real name, but he is, as Mr Maitland surmised, an older man than the prisoner. He is sitting over there,' said Dr Gollnow, pointing to the place where those witnesses who were still present were sitting.

'The gentleman on the left,' said the judge, and made a pretence of consulting his notes. 'Mr Donald Walters, I believe. Would you stand up, Mr Walters, so that the witness can see you clearly?'

MONDAY, After the Verdict

'I am not,' said Sir Nicholas inaccurately, 'a difficult man to please.' Vera and Jenny exchanged glances in which pity for his wrong-headedness and some small anxiety as to what was coming next were nicely blended. 'The matter was handled clumsily, very clumsily indeed, and quite unnecessarily so.'

'But, Uncle Nick, what else could he have done?' Jenny demanded.

'Enough had been said to Chief Inspector Sykes to make him doubtful at least of Mrs Caroline Ryder's guilt in the case he was investigating. We all know him well enough to realise that he wouldn't have allowed it to rest there; he would have continued his investigations, and sooner or later the provenance of the murder weapon would have been discovered.'

'That's just it, Uncle Nick,' said Antony. 'Sooner or later.'

'A case can always be re-opened when there is new evidence to hand,' his uncle pointed out.

'I didn't think that was good enough.'

'You were impatient, a not altogether unfamiliar state of mind. And perhaps you enjoy these sensations of yours.'

'That's very unfair, Uncle Nick,' said Jenny indignantly. 'It wouldn't be good for a young, pregnant woman to have her husband convicted of what's practically treason, let alone for her to be tried herself for murder. She might have had a miscarriage.'

'Then why in heaven's name couldn't Antony say so?'

181

demanded Sir Nicholas, unable to think of any direct way of refuting the good sense of this remark.

'You know perfectly well why he didn't, because he thought it would remind me. Well, he's quite right, it would, only I'm not an ostrich.'

'No, my dear, I'm thankful to say you're not,' said Sir Nicholas, almost benign again. So benign in fact that his nephew gave him a distinctly suspicious look. 'All the same, for anyone wanting a quiet life . . . I still think you enjoy raising the devil, Antony.'

'If you mean what happened in court this morning, I never enjoyed anything less in my life,' said Maitland emphatically. He was looking white and drawn, not at all like a man who had just triumphed in a case that had become a *cause célèbre*.

His tiredness had been obvious to all of them, ever since he arrived home to find his uncle and aunt already upstairs with Jenny, having invited themselves to dinner. Or, more accurately, Sir Nicholas having done so, in the face of Vera's gloomy prognostications that this would probably be the last straw as far as Mrs Stokes was concerned, and that her next move would probably be to give them a month's warning. Characteristically, Sir Nicholas waved that aside, saying confidently, 'You'll deal with it, my dear.'

'Now I had thought,' said Sir Nicholas, 'that you'd be feeling elated about having got what you wanted. Your client acquitted, or so Halloran tells me . . . and all on account of your eloquence,' he added.

'Haven't told us yet what happened after Dr Gollnow's admission,' Vera reminded Antony rather hastily.

'I gather Uncle Nick knows already,' said Antony rather bitterly.

'Yes, but he said he'd rather hear it again from your own lips,' Vera told him. 'And even when this Dr Gollnow started to agree with you it couldn't be regarded as absolutely positive proof — '

182

'I should ' have thought — ' Jenny began, to be interrupted in her turn.

'No, Vera's quite right, love. Halloran could still have put up an argument. By the way, Uncle Nick,' he added with an attempt at a lighter tone, 'both he and Carruthers were very patient with me. I can understand Carruthers, it would be a mixture of fairmindedness and curiosity, and I know Halloran has his share of those qualities too. All the same he was appearing for the prosecution, and he has a distinctly sceptical nature. I thought he might be giving me enough rope to hang myself.'

'Would you have blamed him?' Sir Nicholas inquired.

'No, I was grateful. But I admit to some curiosity myself as to his motive for being so tolerant.'

'Probably no more, my dear boy, than a simple desire to see how far you would go,' said Sir Nicholas. 'But you haven't satisfied Vera's curiosity as to how John Ryder's acquittal came about so quickly.'

'It was Donald Walters' reaction to what Dr Gollnow said. He got to his feet as Carruthers had directed, and then just launched himself towards the witness-box like — like a wild beast, if you'll forgive me for being so trite. He must have felt completely demented, because it was quite obvious he couldn't have reached Gollnow, but he just went to pieces. The ushers grabbed at him, and Gollnow's guards got into the act too. He was shouting something about, 'Is this the thanks I get for helping you?' And then — *per mirabile* — Sykes was there with a couple of constables. Perhaps three or four, I don't remember.'

'Good man,' Vera nodded approvingly.

For the moment, Maitland was lost in his narrative. 'After a bit things calmed down, and Sykes went up to the bench, I think to ask the judge whether he could take Walters away for questioning. But Carruthers said, No, he had some questions for this witness himself. And the upshot was that Walters and Gollnow changed places in the

183

witness-box, and Walters — who seemed to have been a good deal more impressed by my argument than anybody else was — came out with a complete confession both of being the false John Ryder and of having killed Winifred Paull. So there was no need to go on any further. Sykes spirited him away, Dr Gollnow's escort took *him* away with them too, and the judge instructed the jury that there was no case to answer and that they should find the prisoner Not Guilty, which they did forthwith.'

'And you didn't come back to chambers,' Sir Nicholas said very gently.

'No, I . . . I went for a walk.'

'To savour your triumph, no doubt.'

'Not exactly.' There was a long pause. 'Don't you see what I've done?' he added rather desperately.

'Saved Mr and Mrs Ryder a good deal of mental anguish, if nothing else.'

'But there is something else. In saving them . . . you said yourself, Uncle Nick, there could have been other ways.'

'Now what have you got into your head?'

'Dr Boris Gollnow. What do you suppose the powers that be will make of the fact that he lied about John Ryder's identity?'

'I imagine it will make them a little wary of granting him the political asylum he's asked for. But that needn't worry you after all.'

'Well, it does.'

'Come now, Antony, this is foolishness even beyond what I generally expect of you.' Sir Nicholas had become severe. 'To begin with, if you had left the investigation of Winifred Paull's murder to the police, and Caroline Ryder's innocence had eventually been established, it is almost certain that her husband's case would have been reviewed as well. And if this Mr Walter's identity as the false John Ryder was established, Dr Gollnow's duplicity would have been revealed just the same.'

'I know that, but — '

'On the other hand, if he asked for political asylum so that he could become . . . I believe the phrase you used is a double agent,' said Sir Nicholas distastefully. 'If that is the case and he's now sent back to his own country, no harm will come to him. Though why that should worry you I simply cannot see.'

'You've got it all wrong. I tell you I like the fellow.'

'Even an enemy —'

'But I think his application was genuine, I don't think his superiors in Directorate T. knew a thing about it. He'll be killed if he's sent back, or something just as bad, and I think it was fear of that that made him back up Winifred Paull's statement. After all, for all he knew she was a perfectly respectable person and the authorities obvioulsy believed her. If he'd contradicted her they'd just have thought it was a lie; that he'd betrayed Nesbit because he was expendable from the Russian point of view, but he was trying to save Ryder.'

'I don't know how you can be so sure.'

'And I don't know how I can prove it to you or to anybody else. When he finally admitted that my client wasn't the John Ryder he had known, he didn't try to grab the straw I'd held out to him, to say he was doing so from sentimental reasons, or to save innocent people. But there were half a dozen times during my cross-examination when he nearly told me, but each time I could feel his fear of the consequences as though — as though it were my own, and I knew then, with absolute certainty, that if he was sent back it would be the end of him. That if I went on, and finally got the admission I wanted, I was as good as signing his death warrant. Can't you imagine the kind of fuss there's been at the Russian Embassy ever since they knew what he'd done; can't you imagine how they'd like to get their hands on him again? But I went on, what else could I do? John and Carol Ryder have their point of view, after all.'

'So in effect,' said Sir Nicholas pensively, 'you've actually fulfilled the mission you originally turned down, the request that you talk to him?'

'Yes, and a fat lot of use that is now.'

'I'm not so sure. Who was it you were in touch with?'

'Carr.'

'The gentleman who spoke French so badly?'

Antony nodded, a little bewildered by this sudden return to what seemed to him now as the dark ages.

'Phone him now and suggest a meeting for tomorrow. And while you're up, my dear boy,' said Sir Nicholas, seeing his nephew rise with alacrity, immediately cheered by the prospect of action, 'I think we should all benefit from another glass of sherry.'

EPILOGUE

TUESDAY, March 19th

I

A great many things happened the following day, which Maitland spent in chambers. The place was buzzing with yesterday's sensation in court, which Antony put down — incorrectly as it happened — to Willett, who had accompanied him to the Old Bailey, having talked out of turn. Geoffrey, with John Ryder in tow, arrived before ten o'clock, a little reproachful because he hadn't been able to find counsel yesterday. John Ryder was almost embarrassingly grateful, and equally difficult to convince that his wife's release was well on the way but these things took time. There was a telephone call from Kevin O'Brien, sounding reassuringly on the mend, who said succinctly, 'Couldn't have done better myself,' a compliment whose brevity commended it particularly to Maitland in his present mood. By then it was just before eleven o'clock, and Hill, on the inter-office phone, was saying apologetically, 'Mr Carr to see you, Mr Maitland.'

'But I doubt if it was any use,' said Antony to his uncle over lunch. 'He listened of course, but I have a nasty feeling I might as well have been talking double Dutch. Or even French,' he added reminiscently, forgetting for the moment that his uncle was as aware of the fact as he was himself. An almost sleepness night had done little to fix yesterday's events in his mind. 'He once got himself nearly arrested in Pontoise as a matter of fact, for having lecherous designs on

187

a young female. And in peacetime too.'

'And had he?' queried Sir Nicholas, knowing well enough that his nephew was talking at random, but feeling that any distraction was better than none.

'Had he what?'

'Lecherous designs —'

'Good lord, no. Carr is as sober a chap as you can imagine. And talking of imagination, I'm afraid he's a bit short on that too. Which makes it very unlikely that he'd be in sympathy with what I was saying. But that's enough of that,' he added, finishing his whisky at a gulp, at which Sir Nicholas's eyes widened a little. '*Que sera sera*, and there's nothing whatever I can do about it.'

II

Notwithstanding their dinner together the previous evening, the usual Tuesday engagement held good. Vera reported with satisfaction that she'd been able to distract Mrs Stokes's attention from last night's wasted meal, and that there now appeared to be no chance that she would leave them. 'The trouble is, Vera,' said Antony, who was making a great attempt this evening not to allow his own mood to infect the others, 'you've got those two eating out of your hand, and if we ever had any hope of getting rid of Gibbs, Uncle Nick scotched it when he married you.'

'Sorry about that,' said Vera gruffly. 'If you've any ideas as to how I can put that right — '

That was a subject about which none of them was short of ideas, and the conversation grew hilarious. The matter that was uppermost in all their minds wasn't reverted to again until the coffee was poured after dinner, when Sir Nicholas asked idly, 'Has Chief Inspector Sykes been in touch with you today?'

'Yes, he phoned late this afternoon.'

'Will he need a statement from you?'

'Just a formality, he said. Walters saw his solicitor, and repeated the confessions he made in court rather more coherently. He seems to have no idea of pleading anything but Guilty.'

'Was he ever in love with Winifred Paull?' asked Jenny.

'Sykes doesn't think so; it was a matter of convenience.'

'Then why marry her?'

'I don't know the answer to that question for sure, but I should think it was to have access to the bank accounts. He didn't want the one he'd had for years in his own name to reflect any of the payments he'd got from Dr Gollnow.'

'Well, I can see it gave him a hold over her, but surely he put paid to that when he killed her.'

'His second statement explained why he wasn't too worried about that. He was pretty sure Dr Gollnow's defection was a fake, that they'd still be working together, and anyway, as he knew the doctor had committed perjury, he could always put the screws on.'

'Been wondering,' said Vera, 'how did the Chief Inspector explain turning up in court just at the right moment?'

'I didn't think of it at the time, but of course I see now that's what he would naturally do,' Antony told her. 'After our talk on Sunday — '

'Didn't mean to you, meant to Chief Superintendent Briggs.'

'Information received,' said Antony, almost as laconically as Vera herself might have done. 'He said that if Briggs had pressed the matter he'd have talked about an anonymous telephone call, but luckily he didn't have to go as far as that.'

'Bet he knows you were behind it somehow though.'

'I daresay he does, but there's nothing he can do about it. Sykes will get the credit for solving the case brilliantly and preventing a miscarriage of justice, and that's all there is to it.'

But it wasn't quite all. At that moment Gibbs, reverting

for some reason to his old, aggravating habit, stumped upstairs to inform them that there was a foreign gentleman to see Mr Maitland, a Doctor something he thought. He'd put the visitor in the study as Sir Nicholas wasn't using it.

Antony was already half-way to the door when he turned. 'It *could* be Gollnow,' he said. 'Will you come with me, Uncle Nick?'

'My curiosity', said Sir Nicholas, rising languidly to his feet, 'is as great as the next man's. Certainly I will come with you.'

And it was indeed Dr Gollnow, toasting his toes in front of the fire Gibbs must have revived for him. A sign of rare favour, as both Antony and Sir Nicholas knew. 'Mr Maitland,' he said, getting up as the two men came in. 'I trust you will forgive this intrusion, but there were things I wished to say to you.'

'Before you leave?' said Antony unguardedly.

'In a way, but not perhaps in the way you mean.' He paused, looking inquiringly at Sir Nicholas, and Maitland hastily performed the introductions. His uncle waved the visitor to a chair, and offered cognac. A few minutes later, when they were all comfortably seated, Antony asked rather anxiously, 'Are you sure it was safe for you to come?'

The Russian smiled. 'You are thinking that perhaps I have slipped away from my guards, but I assure you that is not the case. They came with me to your door and will return in precisely half an hour to escort me back to my lodgings again.'

'I thought — '

'You thought perhaps that my application for asylum had been turned down, and that I had slipped away from your authorities to become, in fact, a fugitive.'

'Something of the sort,' Antony admitted.

'No. Any danger, I'm sorry to say, would come from my own people. But they do not know where I have been living, they do not know why I should come here. Why should I visit the man who persuaded me, apparently so much against my own interests, into admitting a lie?'

'That's just what I was wondering, Dr Gollnow.'

'Then let me tell you. My application has been approved . . . and if that seems quick to you let me assure you it hasn't been quick at all. It was already decided, when the trial was over, that Boris Gollnow would cease to exist. I should in effect be re-born. Yesterday seemed to have changed all that, but now it seems that nothing is changed, and all, I am told, thanks to you, Mr Maitland.'

'I — '

'Oh, but I am assured of this. You have talked to one of my — may I call them my new friends? — and assured him over and over again of my sincerity. so I have come to thank you.'

Maitland was on his feet, his glass untouched where he had placed it. 'No thanks are necessary,' he said, and seemed to be speaking with difficulty. 'I did what I had to do but it was no pleasure, I assure you, to know that if I succeeded I should be sending you . . . back.'

'Do you think I did not know how you felt? Again and again as we talked . . . but I have done what I came to do, and will not embarrass you any further. Some day perhaps I shall learn to understand you English.'

'What are you going to do?'

'Grow roses perhaps.' That was said with a smile. 'But first I wanted you to know that you were right in what you said of me, that everything I did since I forsook my countrymen . . . everything except that one great lie, was perfectly sincere.' He paused, looking rather wonderingly at Maitland. 'And yet it is not everyone who would have understood how fear can drive a man.'

Antony's lips tightened. 'That is something I understand very well,' he said.

'Even though you, yourself, in my place, would have acted differently?'

'I . . . don't . . . know.'

'You underrate yourself, Mr Maitland. That is

sometimes a mistake. I must leave you now, with my regrets that circumstances will not permit me to further our acquaintance.'

'But — '

'I shall have my new identity.'

'There are too many people here who can recognise you, your colleagues at the Embassy for instance.'

'No, I shall not stay in London or near London. I do not wish to live forever with fear at my heels. But wherever I go . . . I sometimes feel like a boy, that I have the whole world at my feet — '

'With certain exceptions,' said Sir Nicholas rather dryly.

'True, there are places I cannot go, nor would I wish to any longer. And if you are so worried about me, Mr Maitland,' he added, looking up at Antony and smiling again, 'I am, I assure you, a very ingenious person. My tracks will be well hidden.'

'So that was your Russian,' said Sir Nicholas to his nephew as they climbed the stairs together after the visitor had left some ten minutes later.

'There was no need for him to thank me,' said Maitland. 'I was only trying to undo the harm I'd done him.'

'My dear boy, if people tell lies they must take the consequences themselves,' said Sir Nicholas piously. 'All is now well,' he added to Vera and Jenny, flinging open the door and preceding his nephew into the living-room. 'Right has triumphed — or what Antony believes is right,' he couldn't resist adding, 'and we can all forget about the whole sordid affair.'

Jenny looked up at her husband and held out a hand to him. 'They're going to let him stay?' she asked.

'They are, love. And I was so sure . . . but it doesn't matter now. For once you've got your happy ending.' And for once, thought Jenny, looking up at him with compassionate understanding, you, my dearest, are troubled by no doubts at all.

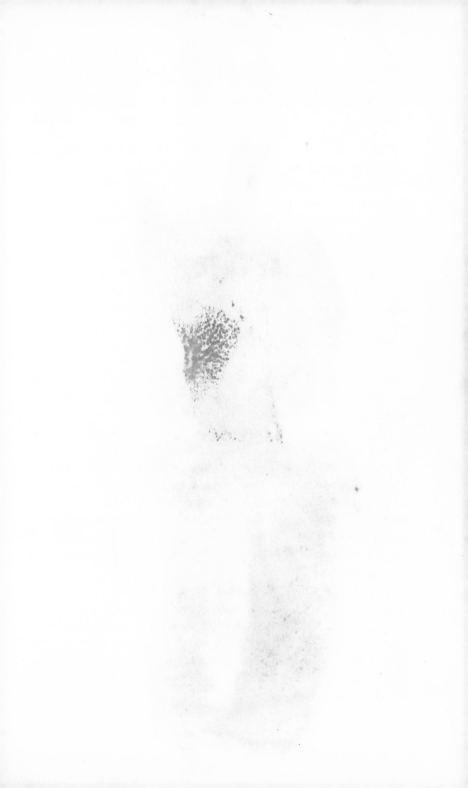